RECON MARINES

P.K. HAWKINS

SEVERED PRESS
HOBART TASMANIA

RECON MARINES

Copyright © 2017 P.K. Hawkins
Copyright © 2017 by Severed Press

WWW.SEVEREDPRESS.COM

ISBN: 978-1-925597-62-2

June 18, 2147 (Earth Calendar)
1433 Greenwich Mean Time
Location: Troop Transport *Franklin Dixon*, Near Ganymede
Marine Heartbeats Detected on Ship: 54

"Bad news, kids," a voice said through the overhead intercom. "Shore leave's been cancelled."

The Recon Marines in the mess hall collectively groaned. Many of them cursed. One of them, although Marsden didn't see who, angrily threw a wad of synthetic mashed potatoes at the wall. Marsden, however, had the opposite reaction. He laughed.

"Told you!" he said to everyone else that had been sitting at his table. "Pay up!"

"Man, you're a sicko," Llewellyn said as she unclipped her personal data monitor from the front of her uniform. "What kind of twisted bastard actually bets against us getting shore leave again?"

"The kind of twisted bastard that knows how things work around here and likes money," Marsden said as he unclipped his own PDM and held it out over the center of the table. "Come on. Mossier, Chunda, you too. I believe that was five hundred scripunits each?" Mossier and Chunda both grumbled as they took out their PDMs, keyed in the amount of money they needed to transfer, and passed them over Marsden's PDM. Once Llewellyn did the same, Marsden checked the PDM's screen to make sure they hadn't shorted him. He had fifteen hundred more scripunits in his personal account now.

"Laugh it up while you can," Chunda grumbled at him. "One

of these days you're going to bet against shore leave, and then you won't be coming back from that particular mission to spend your ill-gotten gains." He put his PDM back and stood up. "See you all at the pods."

Axel, the only other person at Marsden's table, shook her head as the other three left. "I don't understand why they haven't learned yet. The odds of any Recon Marine ever getting to experience a full shore leave are twenty-three to one."

"And when did you have time to calculate those odds?" Marsden asked her with a grin. She cocked her head as if that was the strangest question she had ever heard.

"Just now. Why?"

Marsden just shook his head. He had no doubt that she had indeed just figured that out in her head over the last several seconds, and that she honestly couldn't comprehend why no one else could do the same. Unlike the others, who hadn't bothered to put their lunch trays back into the cleaning unit as a sort of petty revenge at their situation, Marsden and Axel both properly disposed of their trays. A cleaning robot would be around to take care of any mess that got left behind while the marines were all in dilation-sleep, but Marsden felt bad about leaving messes behind for others to clean up, even if the one cleaning was a bot with no programmed personality. Axel, he assumed, took care of her own tray simply because it was the most logical thing to do.

"You sure you don't want to make any bets on what the mission is this time?" Marsden asked Axel as they left the mess hall. Everyone else had already gone and would now either be in their sleep pods or else prepping for them. Marsden didn't see any reason to hurry. Although the ship would be set to jump in the next ten minutes, it had safety features in place that would keep the ship from light jumping if it didn't detect that every living being on board was tucked away safely.

"You don't fool me, Marsden," Axel said. The woman couldn't really be said to have friends, but she said the words with the closest thing she was capable of to affection. "You always win your bets. Always. That sort of thing is statistically impossible, so it stands to reason that you either somehow manipulate the events ahead of time or, as would be more likely in this case, you have some prior knowledge of what is happening."

Marsden kept a straight face. "Don't be silly. How would I know in advance about something like this? Even the command pilots don't know where we're going until minutes before they have to get into their pods."

"I don't know," Axel said. Her tone clearly indicated that she was annoyed that there was something she couldn't figure out. "But it's the only possibility."

When they reached the main sleep pod chamber, Axel silently broke off from him and went one direction to her own pod while Marsden went the other. There were only a few marines that hadn't sealed themselves in their pods yet. Marsden was completely unsurprised to find that Bayne was one of them. Bayne had the oversized pod next to Marsden's. The pod were designed to be as cozy as possible around the marines while they were in dilation sleep, which meant that there had to be several different size pods to accommodate them all. Marsden's was the average size, and Axel's was among the smallest that the Recon Marines provided. Bayne's was the biggest, and according to rumor had to be custom ordered, as none of the off-the-shelf models would fit his height and shoulder-width.

"Marsden," Bayne said in his typical deep rumble of a voice. "Did she..."

"No," Marsden said with a sigh.

"I didn't even finish the question. How would you know what I was going to ask?"

"Because it's the same damned question you always ask. No, Axel didn't ask or say anything about you."

"Nothing? Nothing at all?"

"Bayne, when are you going to give this up? Axel's not into you."

"You think she's into someone else?" Bayne asked. For such a huge, intimidating man, he somehow managed to look very much like a scolded puppy.

"As far as I can tell, she's not into anyone. I've never, ever seen her show any sort of romantic or sexual interest in anyone of any gender. I don't even get why you're so into her. There are plenty of women in the Recon Marines who would be more than happy to hook up with you."

"I don't want someone to hook up with. I want someone to connect with."

"You have the body of a steel pillar," Marsden said. He refrained from adding that Bayne also had the brains of one. "She has the body of a petite gymnast. She has the brain of a calculator. You, uh, don't. What do you possibly think the two of you could connect over?"

"We both like explosions."

Marsden had to shrug at that. They did indeed both like explosions. The difference was that for Bayne, it was an occasional diverting fling, while for Axel, it was a passionate love affair for the ages. There was a reason Axel was the explosive expert on the ship. Bayne was more of the heavy artillery type.

Once they had both finished their prep for the pods, Marsden got into his, pressed the button to close and seal it, then took a deep whiff of the fast-acting sleeping gas that flooded the chamber. He lost all consciousness for what felt like a mere five seconds for him, then a second gas pumped into the pod to wake him up. The pod opened and he carefully got out. Bayne did the same beside him, although the enormous man stumbled and almost fell.

"I hate that," Bayne said. "Remind me again why we have to do that every single time the ship makes a jump?"

"Maybe because we don't want to die or go insane?" Marsden asked.

"Right," Bayne said. "There is that, I guess."

Personally, Marsden had to wonder if Bayne's abnormally sized sleep pod didn't pump in enough gas each time, and it caused light brain damage on each jump, because he always asked that question every time. Marsden always gave the exact same answer, and Bayne always acted like he was hearing Marsden's smartass remark for the first time.

The pods existed for two reasons. The first was to protect their bodies from the harsh and unusual forces working on the ship during a light jump. The second was to keep them from losing their minds from the jump's weird time effects.

To everyone now leaving their pods and starting to suit up for the mission, it felt like only a matter of seconds had passed since they'd gotten in their pods. The actual time that would have passed according to the *Dixon*'s ship-board computer would have been anywhere between ten and fifteen minutes. And yet, the time that would have passed outside the ship, according to the standard Earth calendar, would be anywhere from two to three weeks, depending on how far exactly they had traveled. The light-jump caused time dilation effects, thanks to Einstein's Special Theory of Relativity. It was why Recon Marines were encouraged not to have too many friends and loved ones outside the service: to anyone back on the core planets, the people on these ships were barely aging, while to the people on the *Dixon*, everyone else aged slightly faster.

Marsden went to his equipment locker to get his gear. As he did, his PDM chirped right along with everyone else's. Marsden didn't bother to unclip his and look at it, as enough people around him were doing it that he could hear everything their incoming message said.

"Good day, marines," a gruff voice said from multiple PDMs. If Marsden had actually been looking at his instead of inspecting his helmet and light armor, he knew he would see an extreme close-up of a mustachioed man's face looking out at him through a static-filled blue screen. The Recon Marines tended to simply call the man Mister, although there was plenty of debate as to whether Mister existed at all or was just some computer program that sent them their orders for each mission. "As you receive this message, the current time is"—Mister's voice was completely replaced for a second by a different, more obviously computer-generated voice—"1647 Greenwich Mean Time, August 2nd, 2147 Earth calendar."

Marsden paused in shrugging into his light armor, unsure that he had heard the date correctly. He almost thought it was just him, but the woman who had a locker next to his, Murakame, spoke up.

"Almost two months? Just how far exactly did we travel?"

It was a rhetorical question that no one bothered to answer. If they'd lost nearly two months instead of the standard two weeks, either something had gone wrong with the engines to make them go slower, or else they had travelled farther into the galaxy than any of them had ever been before. The first possibility was extremely unlikely, given how paranoid the Recon Marine techs were about making sure everything on the ship ran smoothly, so it was probably the second option.

A murmur passed through the marines as they registered this. A few sounded audibly nervous, while most of the others were excited. This was the kind of thing they'd signed up with the Recon Marines for, after all. If they'd wanted easy, safe jobs, they would have signed up for one of the core planet military branches or militias.

"You are all here because the Recon Marines have enacted the Elliot Contingency."

Marsden whistled. Wow, this was a big one. It was a good thing he hadn't bet Axel where they were going after all. He would have lost this one big time.

"What's the Elliot Contingency?" Bayne asked, a little too loudly, from his own locker. While Mister's speech had been pre-recorded before they'd even been sent out, Marsden smiled at the way Mister seemed to anticipate Bayne's question.

"For those of you too lazy or illiterate to read your damned manuals," Mister said. "The Elliot Contingency is for when first contact is anticipated with a potentially hostile alien race."

"Wow, really?" a grunt named Nunez said from a few lockers down. "What does that put us at now?"

"If we confirm their presence," Axel called out from somewhere, "this would be the sixth sentient and intelligent non-human species we have made contact with." What she didn't say was that only two of them, so far, had been anything close to friendly toward humans. Although it might not be the best politics, the Recon Marines pretty much assumed by this point that they needed to be ready for hostile.

Mister continued while everyone finished gearing up. "On Earth Calendar May 28th, an automated deep-galactic probe returned to the outpost on Charon with data on several planets possibly capable of supporting human life. Before that information could be passed on to the Colonization Council, an anomaly was detected on the surface of a rocky and arid planet with the current temporary designation of Bullfinch-2.

"Further study of the data revealed the anomaly to be some kind of non-naturally occurring object suggestive of a ship design, although it is one that doesn't match any known design used by the known sentient species. Further data suggests energy patterns consistent with advanced weapon systems, although at this point that is mostly speculation. Command has determined that you marines are to use Pattern 37 in starting to approach the possible vessel, with pattern changes to be determined by M. Dollarhyde and R. Popkess at their discretion. Thus ends the briefing. Good luck, marines." The message ceased, and the image of the man with the mustache disappeared from all their PDMs.

"Alright, everyone, you heard Mister!" Popkess called out from the far end of the lockers. "Everyone designated for planet-fall as part of Pattern 37 needs to be fully prepped and ready in five minutes. Welcome to Bullfinch-2!"

Dollarhyde finished the traditional starting speech of Recon Marine missions. "Why do we do this, everyone?"

Every single marine in the room answered in unison. "Because no one else will!"

"Damned right," Popkess called out. "Now get your asses moving."

August 2, 2147 (Earth Calendar)
1701 Greenwich Mean Time
Location: *Franklin Dixon* Dropship Alpha, Approaching Bullfinch-2
Marine Heartbeats Detected on Dropship: 46

Pattern 37 required that the marines aboard the *Dixon* split into three separate groups. The first and smallest consisted of eight marines that stayed on the main ship. These would be the last resort and included everyone absolutely necessary to get the *Franklin Dixon* back to the core worlds as well as a few support crew like medics in case anyone that came back to the ship needed medical attention that the field medics hadn't been able to administer. The remaining marines split into two groups of twenty-three and huddled together in the main dropship as it fell to the surface of Bullfinch-2. Marsden was in Charlie group under Dollarhyde. He much preferred being under her command than having to deal with Popkess, who had a tendency to talk purely to hear his own voice. Bayne ended up in Delta group and desperately wanted to find someone in Charlie that would switch with him, although that wasn't because he had a problem with Popkess. He simply wanted to be in the same group as Axel, who was sitting quietly on the Charlie side.

"This sucks, Marsden," Bayne said. "Come on, be a friend for once."

"First, stop using the 'be a friend' thing. It might be more believable if you ever let yourself have friends. Second, you know the starting team assignments are based on evenly balancing our knowledge and skills until the team leaders decide to switch it up for mission reasons. If Popkess and Dollarhyde know that you're trying to switch, they'll have your head."

Bayne grunted. "I'm not afraid of Popkess."

"But you are afraid of Dollarhyde."

"Damn right I am. That woman is scary when she's angry."

That was apparently reason enough to get Bayne to be quiet about it for the rest of the trip down. After several minutes of flight, all of their PDMs chirped, and as one the marines pulled them out to look at the screens. While Dollarhyde wasn't sitting so far away from Marsden that he couldn't see or hear her, it was standard pre-mission procedure for the mission's commanders to use the PDMs just to make sure that every single marine on the dropship clearly got everything she was saying.

"Okay, listen up," Dollarhyde said. "The tac/tech strategists on this one are going to be Mingo on Charlie team and Arizona on Delta team. Arizona, do the honors and show us what you two have picked up so far."

Dollarhyde's image on the screen was replaced with a small inset of Arizona and a much larger scan of the planet's surface. "Bullfinch-2 is currently getting classified as a Class C environment." Marsden didn't need her to explain that this meant it was capable of supporting human life, but hardly the kind of place anyone would want to stay for long. Most Class C planets didn't even have their own native life. "Tox and microbe scans are currently showing negative, but as is standard procedure for a class C, continue to wear your mini re-breathers until we give the okay otherwise. Our destination is here." A point lit up in a mountainous area on the screen, then zoomed in for a closer shot of the target. The ship in question was resting on a plateau, although the long gouge in the rock and trail of debris behind it implied that it hadn't had the most majestic of landings. "Mingo, you're the one who know more about alien design," Arizona said.

"Tell us what you're seeing here."

Mingo's picture replaced Arizona's. "The rounded, lengthy design of the ship is reminiscent of the warships used by the Stenani, but random bulbous regions up and down the side do not match anything we've seen for any other known race. It's possible that we're dealing with some offshoot of the Stenani, although we won't be able to know for sure until we get inside."

Llewellyn's picture appeared briefly at the bottom of the screen as she asked a question. "That ship looks dead. Are we anticipating anything alive in there?"

Arizona's picture appeared again. "We're reading no life signs on board, although we're picking up some kind of interference we've never seen before, so we're going to make the assumption that there could still be something dangerous in there until we see otherwise. Given the amount of dust and weathering we're seeing on the ship's hull, we're making the rough estimate that it has been here for about three years. Chances of survivors under those conditions are slim, but we can't be sure without knowing anything of the capabilities of the species that made it."

Dollarhyde came back on in Arizona's place. "Dropship Alpha will land here," she said as a red point appeared on the map roughly two hundred meters to the east of the ship. "Charlie team will proceed north around what we believe is the aft of the ship and then west to a breach we've detected in the hull. Delta team will go directly west to what we believe may be the main entrance."

Popkess replaced Dollarhyde. "Our main objective is to determine if there are any alien life forms present. If we find nothing alive, then we secure the site and send an all-clear to the Science Corps. If we do find something alive, you are not to engage *unless attacked*. We all know what happened the last time some jackass got too trigger happy. The last thing the Recon Marines need at this point is a repeat of the battle of Alpha Centauri-A. Remember that you are being monitored and will be disciplined if it is determined that you acted aggressively in a situation that did not merit it."

There were mumbles and grumbles all around. Marsden knew from experience that any disciplinary action meted out wouldn't compare to the utter horror that was the mountain of paperwork they would have to fill out if anyone witnessed such a thing. Nothing was more effective at policing itchy trigger fingers than other grunts afraid of red tape.

"However, if the situation does merit it," Dollarhyde added. "Be prepared to sweep the site clean."

That elicited a much more appreciative murmur from the group.

"Does anyone have any other questions?" Popkess asked.

"Yeah," Bayne muttered to himself. "Why is your voice so annoying?"

"I heard that Bayne," Popkess said. "Next time you want to insult your current commander, maybe you should make sure your personal mic isn't recording everything you say. I hope you're prepared for extra cleaning duty when we get back to the *Dixon*."

Bayne frowned, but for once he was smart enough to keep his mouth shut.

"Five minutes to landing," Dollarhyde called out, no longer bothering to use her PDM. Everyone took that as the sign to stow their PDMs and do any final checks needed on their gear. Bayne turned around in his seat to make sure that his heavy chain gun was securely fastened to his back. Axel had her standard MH-56 rifle in hand, but she tended not to use it if she could. Her speed and small size made her much more effective with smaller weapons that she could take with her into tight spaces. More importantly to her, she had pockets full of various explosive devices at convenient places all over her armor.

Marsden didn't have anything special in terms of weapons. He simply had his MH-56, two pistols as side arms, and a knife in his boot. His specialty had less to do with his weapons than with his ability to operate nearly any machinery or transport in a pinch. If either of the pilots were to suddenly drop dead here and now, he would be the one expected to land them safely. He might not be able to guarantee that the touchdown would be pretty, but he would have no problem making one of his bets that everyone on board would live.

Dropship Alpha made planet fall with no problems, however, and the teams immediately filed down the boarding ramp and formed up. The two pilots stayed on the dropship, keeping ready for a speedy exit in the event of an emergency. That left twenty-two people per team, and both Popkess and Dollarhyde took a moment to make sure everyone in their team looked prepped and ready.

While they did this, Marsden took stock of the environment around them. They were in a rocky mountainous region, but given what little they'd been told about the planet, he suspected that most of Bullfinch-2 was like that. All of the marines had put on the half-mask re-breathers that covered the lower part of their face to filter out environmental contaminants, but even through the mask he could feel how thin the air was. The sky was a purplish color despite the local star high in the sky, and there was a small moon hanging on the horizon. Actually, compared to some of the places they'd had to go in the past, this planet wasn't really that bad.

"Alright, let's move out!" Dollarhyde said to Charlie team,

and they all started their march toward the ship. They kept a defensive posture, but Dollarhyde hadn't yet given any signal that they needed to worry yet. All of the marines carefully watched their surroundings, fully aware that, if the crashed ship had indeed had survivors, they could be hiding in the surrounding ridges and preparing an ambush. But their approach to the north side of the ship was uneventful.

The ship had appeared strange enough to their human eyes from the picture they'd seen on their PDMs, but up close Marsden wasn't sure what to make of it. They all assumed they were going around the rear side, but there was nothing there that indicated any mode of propulsion. Some of the bulbous areas could have been weapons, but otherwise they didn't appear to have any purpose. The entire ship looked like a gigantic white cigar covered in tumors.

It took them nearly half an hour just to reach the halfway point of the ship. Here there was an enormous gash in the side that was several stories tall.

"What do you think caused that?" one of the marines asked.

"Looks like it scraped up against one of the mountains when it crashed," someone else said.

The hole in the side was about fifty meters long and about three meters above them. Marsden figured that they would easily be able to climb up the side and find their way in, but Dollarhyde held up her hand in a gesture for them to stay back for the moment.

"Popkess, do you read?" Dollarhyde said into her PDM.

"Read you," Popkess replied.

"We're in position. How about you?"

"We're here, but Arizona and L'wongo are having trouble figuring out how to open the door."

Arizona's voice now came over the PDMs. "There's some kind of interface here, but the power is down. It looks like it's been that way for quite some time now. We're looking for some kind of manual release."

Mingo, who was standing several marines down from Marsden, spoke into his own PDM. "Are there any markings?"

"Yeah," Arizona said. "And just like the rest of the ship, they look similar but still different from Stenani writings."

Marsden piped in. He was rather pleased with himself that he had something to offer at this juncture. "On a Stenani ship, there would usually be depression above the door. It would be about fist sized. That would be their version of a manual release."

"Fat lot of good that would do us," Popkess said. "This door is twice the height of Bayne. None of us would be able to reach it."

"Hold up," Arizona said. "Just because there's similarities to a Stenani ship doesn't mean that a release would be in exactly the same place."

"Over here!" Marsden heard someone else say through the PDMs. "There seems to be something like what Marsden described over by the side of the door."

There was a pause while Charlie team waited for Delta team to try it out. "It's not doing anything," Popkess said. "You got any other great ideas over there, Marsden?"

"Wait, here's another one on the other side," Arizona said. "It doesn't seem to be working either, but maybe if we tried both at once?"

After another pause, there was a whooshing sound from the other end of the PDMs, followed by several whoops of celebration.

"Can it, everyone," Popkess said. "Big deal. We managed to

get a door open. If you're waiting for a medal, you're going to have to wait longer."

Marsden smiled as he heard a familiar voice grumbling. It wasn't loud enough that the PDMs picked up exactly what he said, but Popkess apparently didn't have the same problem.

"I heard that, Bayne. Now not only do you have to do extra cleaning duties, but you're going to have to do all the toilets as well. Now, would you like to get stuck on onion peeling duty as well, or are you ready to shut up?"

Bayne didn't say anything at all.

"Good answer," Popkess said. "Okay then, Dollarhyde. You and your team ready?"

"We've been ready," Dollarhyde said. "If you take any damned longer, I think Axel is going to start getting twitchy and just blow holes in the side of the ship just for the hell of it."

Marsden looked over at Axel, who shrugged at him as if to say, *Maybe*.

Popkess didn't sound too pleased with Dollarhyde's sass, but the other team leader he couldn't punish Dollarhyde for talking back to him like he did his own people.

"Fine then," Popkess said. "Let's go in and see what there is to see."

August 2, 2147 (Earth Calendar)
1759 Greenwich Mean Time
Location: Interior of Unknown Alien Spacecraft,
Bullfinch-2
Marine Heartbeats Detected on Planet: 46

Charlie team carefully climbed up into the rift in the hull and then again waited patiently while Mingo did another scan. "Still no life signs detected, although the interference we were getting earlier is much stronger."

"What could be causing it?" Dollarhyde asked.

"Not a clue," Mingo said. "It's some kind of radiation or energy we haven't encountered before."

Marsden heard Arizona comment through the PDMs. "And the technology isn't matching anything of the intelligence we have on file regarding the Stenani. So either this is something they've been keeping so secret they've somehow managed to keep it from the Galactic Intelligence Agency, or else this truly is a completely new race."

"If this energy is the product of some new technology, then it has to be residual rather than active," Mingo said. "Because it doesn't look like there's any power going to anything in this ship."

"Never make assumptions," Axel muttered nearby. "That's how you end up with false data." Neither Mingo nor Dollarhyde seemed to hear her. They were both too busy doing further scans while Marsden and the others took in their new environment.

They were in some kind of storage, from Marsden's best guess, although it was impossible to be sure. The room was long and narrow with organic, uneven corners. They made Marsden think that the ship might not have been built, but possibly grown in some way. A couple of marines slowly crept up to the walls to take a closer look, but they didn't get too close. For all anyone knew, there were security measures built into the ship that would kill them if they touched anything.

Dollarhyde described everything they saw to Delta team, who in turn gave them a description of their own area. The main entry was apparently cleaner, since it was absent the dirt and dust that had blown in over the years through the gaping hole, but it was otherwise very similar in design.

"Now we're definitely starting to look different than the Stenani," Mingo said.

"No immediate threats detected," Dollarhyde said. "Popkess, we're going to head right in the hopes of finding a command deck or control room. You and your people head to your right and see if you can find anything resembling an engine room or power supply."

"Roger that," Popkess said.

Mingo and several others used their PDMs to map the area around them and their route as the marines cautiously filed out into the hallway, all of them keeping their weapons ready at all times. The rest of the ship was done in the same organic design as the first room, and while they passed a number of rooms, neither Marsden nor any of the others could identify the purpose of most of them. For the next five minutes of slowly proceeding through the corridors, they found nothing of interest. From the bits of chatter that they picked up from Delta team, they seemed to be finding much of the same. It was almost creepy, how little they were finding. If the ship had truly crashed, Marsden would have thought there would be bodies of the crew scattered around.

The first body they found was right in the middle of the

hallway when they turned a corner. Dollarhyde signaled them all to stop for a few minutes, then silently directed them to take up positions around the body. If she was expecting other members of the crew to pop out, however, she would be disappointed. This was the only sign they had found so far that the ship had been inhabited at any point.

"Delta team, we've found a body," Dollarhyde said into her PDM. "Presumably it was one of the crew. Looks like he or she has been dead for quite a while."

The reply that came back from Popkess was broken and fuzzy. "—that again? We're... hearing you."

"Must be the energy interference that's messing with our instruments," Mingo said to Dollarhyde. "There must be enough of whatever it is between our two teams that it's starting to mess with the communications."

"Crap," Dollarhyde said. "What about life sign monitors? Are we still able to pick those up?"

"Those broadcast on a different wavelength," one of the other marines next to Mingo said. "So far they don't seem to be affected."

"Thank God for small favors," Dollarhyde said. "Popkess, did you catch any of that?"

"Some," Popkess said. "Your video feed... not giving enough details, so I can't... Please repeat... originally said."

"I said we've found a body. Dead for a long time. Have you found anything similar yet?"

"Negative. In fact..." The rest of his sentence was cut off by static.

"Say again, Popkess."

"I said it's a... how clean it is. We're not... biological material at all. Like something... -eaning the whole area on a..."

"I think I picked up enough of that to understand what he's saying," Dollarhyde said. "Mingo, Chunda, you two probably have the most xenobiology knowledge among us. Take a look at this body and tell us what you see."

Both Mingo and Chunda kneeled down next to the body. Marsden couldn't help his curiosity. He moved slightly out of position to get a better view of the two as they examined the alien remains.

"Definitely not a Stenani," Mingo said.

"No, but the basic shape has a lot of similarities," Chunda said. "I think you were right that we might be dealing with something related. Maybe it's some kind of evolutionary offshoot. If the Stenani weren't so hostile to humans, we might be able to ask them about this."

"But the Stenani are hostile," Dollarhyde said. "So we're going to go with the assumption that if any of these things are still alive in here, they're going be out for our blood."

"Why isn't it decayed at all?" one of the marines asked. "If a body had just been sitting here for years, wouldn't it be nothing but bones by now? Or at least mummified, or something like that?"

"Actually, it *is* nothing but bones," Mingo said as he gently nudged the body with the toe of his boot. It moved very easily, as if the whole thing was light from being hollow. "I think we're looking at an exoskeleton."

"Like an insect?" Marsden asked. "The Stenani don't have exoskeletons, do they?"

"No, they don't," Chunda said. "And that's a pretty huge difference between Stenani biology and what we're seeing here. They have skeletons like we do. Evolutionarily, we shouldn't be seeing something with an exoskeleton and the typical Stenani features like the beak and the skinny limbs. I would almost guess that this guy was some kind of genetically altered mutant or hybrid."

"I'm not seeing anything on the body that looks like a weapon," Dollarhyde said.

"I don't either," Chunda said. "I am seeing this, though." He pointed out several holes in the exoskeleton that were about the width of Marsden's thumb. "Conway, want to come take a look at this?"

Conway, Charlie team's medic on this mission, came forward and gave the holes a closer inspection.

"What do they look like to you?" Dollarhyde asked her. "Some kind of weapons damage? Was it shot?"

"No, I don't think so, at least not from any kind of weapon we would recognize. If this had been caused by a bullet, the bullet would still either be in the body or somewhere nearby. And I don't see any bullet holes in the walls or shell casings nearby."

"What about an energy weapon of some kind?" Chunda asked.

Mingo shook his head. "The only alien race that we've confirmed has been able to develop real working energy weapons so far are the Manises. And they only have them as a deterrent against other races attacking them. The Manises consider themselves to be peaceful and neutral."

"And even if they weren't," Conway said, "I'm willing to bet such a weapon would leave some kind of darkened scoring mark." She sharply looked up at Marsden. "It's just an expression, Marsden. Don't you dare try to con me out of any of my money."

Marsden held up the hand that wasn't holding his rifle in a "don't look at me" gesture. "Wouldn't dream of it," he said.

"Yeah, right," Conway mumbled, then turned back to the

body. "But do you see these tiny marks around the holes? If I had to guess, I would say those are teeth marks of some kind."

"Teeth marks?" Dollarhyde asked. "Something ate it?"

"Something rather small, by the looks of it," Conway said. "Although I don't think it's something we need to be worried about. It just means that Bullfinch-2 isn't as devoid of native life as we thought. It has its scavengers."

"I don't know," Mingo said. "The life scans on the way here looked pretty empty."

"It's not going to matter," Dollarhyde said to them. "Something that small's not going to pose any threat to us. Popkess, I hope you've been hearing all this?"

The PDMs popped and crackled with static, but there was no other response.

"Popkess? Talk to us. Can you still hear us on this end?"

There was a long pause before Popkess answered. "Holy hell, Dollarhyde. You guys need to see what we're seeing."

All of their PDMs lit up with a live feed from Popkess's camera. Just like their video feed to Popkess, there were enough breaks in the signal that it was hard to watch. At first it was hard to tell what they were seeing, as there was no sense of scale. All they could see were the dark walls with blue spots against them. It wasn't until the camera caught a couple of marines in the shot that Marsden realized how large some of these bubbles were. They were opaque and bright in color, a contrast so stark against the plain black walls that the bubbles seemed to glow. They protruded out of the walls much like the formations on the outside of the ship.

"Popkess, where are you?" Dollarhyde asked. "What exactly are these things?"

"Damned if I know, Dollarhyde. You probably can't see it

through the camera, but this room is huge and there's maybe fifty of these blue things scattered about it."

"Your feed is coming through stronger now. Did you guys do something to stop the interference?"

"No, that's the weirdest thing," Arizona chimed in. "Not only are all of our devices working perfectly fine again, but when we tried to scan these blue things, they picked up nothing. Not even anything in the background. A complete blank on all readouts."

"Which means what, exactly?" Dollarhyde asked.

"I don't know for sure," Arizona said. "But my best guess is that these things are somehow responsible for our signals getting clearer. Or maybe they were the reason for the interference. Or maybe…"

Dollarhyde sighed. "Quit giving me maybes and give me a definite."

"Okay, fine. This blue stuff is definitely maybe responsible for something. Or not."

"Thanks a lot, Arizona, that was a big help," Mingo said wryly.

"That's me. Little Miss Helpful."

While everyone else had been engaged in the banter, Marsden had been paying close attention to any detail he could see of the bubbles. Something caught his eye, and he spoke up. "Popkess, wait. Move your camera back just a little bit to that last bubble."

"There's nothing to see, Marsden," Popkess said.

"Do what he says," Dollarhyde said. She looked at Marsden with a raised eyebrow. "So? What did you think you saw?"

"It looked like there was a shadow on the bubble," Marsden said.

Arizona came into the frame once Popkess had the camera aimed back at the bubble. "Marsden's right," Arizona said.

"Except I don't think it's a shadow on the bubble. I think it's a shadow *in* the bubble. There's something inside here." Arizona turned away out of the shot, but they could all still hear her. "There's something inside all of them. I can't see what, though."

Popkess turned the camera back to his own face. "We definitely need to come back and take a better stock of this room, but I don't think this is where we should be spending all of our time."

"I agree," Dollarhyde said. "Both teams should converge on that room for further study. But for now we still need you to keep heading to the back of the ship and catalog everything you see. Keep trying to find some kind of engine room and see what you can do about restoring power. Just watch your back. For as long as we don't know what those blue things are, treat them like they're potentially dangerous."

"Hell, probably a good idea to treat everything in here like a potential danger," Popkess said.

"Roger that," Dollarhyde responded. "Keep going and remain in contact."

The video feed from Popkess's group clicked off.

"Okay then," Dollarhyde said to the rest of Charlie team. "Conway, are you about finished with your examination of the body?"

"For now. We're going to have to bag it and tag, though. There's no way we're not taking this thing back with us. The Science Corps would have our heads if we failed to get them some kind of sample of a new sentient alien race."

"We can't go hauling it around with us," Dollarhyde said. "It'll keep just fine here until we head on back. Alright everyone, form back up and move out. We've still got to find the br—"

All of their PDMs buzzed at the same time. Marsden grabbed

his again, expecting it to light back up with another video feed from Delta team. Instead it was flashing red with a single message.

MARINE HEARTBEATS DETECTED ON PLANET: 45

"Oh hell," Conway said. She quickly looked around at Charlie team like she was expecting to see that one of them had inexplicably dropped dead. Marsden did a visual count at the same time she did. Everyone was accounted for. There were still twenty-two people here.

The PDMs buzzed again, and the message changed.

MARINE HEART BEATS DETECTED ON PLANET: 44

And then again.

MARINE HEART BEATS DETECTED ON PLANET: 43

It was only then that the red message was replaced once more with the video feed. Instead of a shot of the bubbles, though, it was now a picture of Popkess's face, panic-stricken and covered in blood.

"They're everywhere!" he screamed. "They're coming for—"

The video was abruptly replaced with static, and then cut off completely as the red message returned.

MARINE HEART BEATS DETECTED ON PLANET: 42

August 2, 2147 (Earth Calendar)
1828 Greenwich Mean Time
Location: Corridor of Unknown Alien Spacecraft,
Bullfinch-2
Marine Heart Beats Detected on Planet: 41

Dollarhyde no longer bothered to watch as the number continued to drop. "Everyone, defensive formation and keep heading for the front of the ship."

"Wait, what?" one of the marine's yelled. "You can't really expect us to go the opposite direction from them! Something's killing them! We have to go find them."

"And by the time we do find them," Marsden said, "whatever did it will probably be finished with them and ready for us to provide it with a few fresh kills."

"Marsden's right," Dollarhyde said. "All we know is that there is something deadly in that direction. And if we're going to have any chance of helping any survivors, then we need to be alive and in a safe, defensible position first. So stop questioning my orders and move!"

Although there was a distinct franticness to their movements, all of Charlie team remained poised and ready as they raised their rifles against any possible threat that might come out of the darkness. With renewed caution and speed, they all continued down the corridor in search of some position that would be easy to defend if something came for them. While this was happening, Mingo continued to call out the heartbeat count as they went, finally stopping at thirty-nine.

"Whatever was happening back there, it seems like it might be over," he said.

"Jesus," Conway said softly. "I don't know what that was, but something just killed seven highly experienced Recon Marines in less than two minutes."

"We should try to reestablish communications with them," Llewellyn said.

"Negative," Dollarhyde responded. "Not only do we need to make sure that Charlie team is in a safe position first, but we don't know the circumstances are for the remaining sixteen members of Delta team. If they're in hiding and trying to remain quiet, any sound from us trying to talk to them might give them away. Once we're in a good position we'll wait several minutes and see if any of them reach out to us."

They continued down the hall in a tight formation, passing a number of doors and side halls that often appeared to be there for no reason at all. They continued to let their equipment map the ship as they went, but that was no longer their number one priority. It was more a necessity of survival now: every nook and cranny could be the hidey-hole of some potential enemy, and they still had no clue what form that enemy might take.

"Sensors seem to indicate that the hall leads onto a very large room ahead," Mingo said. "It could be the bridge or control room."

"Or it could be their version of the bathroom, for all we know," Dollaryhyde said. "Let's get our asses in there and take stock of it. If it's defensible, that's where we set up shop. If not, then we have to find something else."

As they came into the room, Marsden whistled. "Okay, bet time. I'm putting fifty scripunits on this being the bridge."

"Okay, new order," Dollarhyde said to the whole group. "Any idiot who bets against Marsden on anything at all gets extra cleaning duties back on the ship right along with Bayne. The last thing I need right now is for anyone to be too worried about the status of their bank accounts while we're fighting for our lives."

Marsden shook his head. "You're no fun."

The room they had come into had much taller ceilings than anything else they had seen in the ship thus far, and one wall was mostly covered in a flat, jelly-like surface. Two sets of awkwardly placed stairs led up to a raised dais, where a number of stools designed to support distinctly inhuman anatomy were placed alongside bulging, organic mounds full of depressions and holes. Looking around, Marsden saw that there was a second entrance into the room, but those two doors seemed to be the only ways in or out.

"This actually looks perfect," Dollarhyde said. "Mingo and Chunda, scan the room for anything that might be a threat. Life signs, strange power readings, anything at all. I don't want to get blindsided just because we're unfamiliar with how these aliens think."

Even being as thorough as possible, Mingo and Chunda reported in only a few minutes that the entire area seemed to be clean of threats. There was another exoskeleton body hunched over the central stool on the dais, though, and from its size compared to the other one, Marsden suspected that this one had been the leader or captain of the ship. The alien captain looked like he had suffered the same fate as the one they'd found in the hall, with several holes evident in the exoskeleton where something had eaten through to get at whatever soft flesh might have been underneath. Conway did note, however, that there seemed to be fewer holes, although she couldn't say for certain what that meant.

"Okay then, this is where we're setting up until we find out what happened to Delta team," Dollarhyde said. "Axel and Zhou, you two get to work setting up traps at those two doors that we can set off if something other than our own people come through them. Marsden and Mingo, those weird mound things might be controls or something. See what you can figure out about them. Conway, get to work analyzing any data that came through the PDMs regarding what happened to Delta team. Everyone else, we're taking advantage of that raised dais to get a get some height on whatever may come for us. Set up in a defensive posture, concentrating any possible fire on the two doors and the two sets of stairs as choke points. I want anything non-human that comes through those doors to be Swiss cheesed with bullets before it gets anywhere near us."

Marsden and Mingo immediately set about examining the strange mounds near the stools. They didn't look anything at all like controls as humans would understand them, but just like the depressions that had been used to open the main door, these things looked like they had similarities to Stenani design. As Marsden took a knee to get a closer look at them, Conway announced the information that had come through the PDMs.

"The PDMs have lost life signs for Popkess, L'Wongo, Schiltz, Xavier, Kransky, Murdock, and Virgo."

Marsden did his best not to be distracted by this news. All Recon Marines were comrades and would fight and die for each other, but actual friendships were discouraged for exactly this reason. They could die at any instant, and that would provide a distraction to anyone who'd become too close to them. And distractions would only lead to more deaths. Still, there were several among those names that Marsden had particularly liked, and although none of them were friends, he'd been through a lot with them.

The time to mourn them was later, though. For now he

needed to concentrate on the task at hand.

"They're also showing weakened life signs from Murakame, Graznow, and Lochner. Jesus, and those are just the injuries significant enough to make an impact on their heartbeats and brain waves. Whatever hit them really chewed them up."

"Hmmm," Dollarhyde mumbled to herself. "We need to get in contact with them and know what happened, but don't send anything that will make a noise and possibly give away their position. Send a request for information by text, and make sure it's properly coded for security. Don't make any assumptions about who or what the enemy might be until we have further information."

"Got it," Conway said. While she went about this task, Mingo came over to join Marsden.

"Make anything of it?" Mingo asked him.

"Probably just as much as you do," Marsden said. "Similar to Stenani design but different. Given that the front door required two separate people at opposite ends to open it, we should be aware that a similar dynamic might be needed here to operate any of this. What's this, though?" Marsden asked, indicating some markings that swirled in and around the depressions with no apparent rhyme or reason.

Mingo pulled out his PDM and used it to scan the markings. "Instructions or labels on how to use all this, hopefully. We'll see what my translating software can do with it. Given that it does have a lot in common with Stenani, that should make the translation faster. If it needed to translate a brand new alien language completely from scratch, that would take much longer."

All of their PDMs buzzed with an incoming video feed. Dollarhyde immediately took charge of the conversation. "Delta team, do you read? Tell us what's going on."

Arizona's face appeared on their screens. Her helmet was now missing, and there was a massive, jagged scratch down her cheek along with blood leaking out from her nose. Her eyes were wide and she was very obviously scared, but her tone remained cool and even as she talked. "We didn't see any of them at first. They just blended in with the walls, and even when we did see them they seemed too small to be a threat."

Most of the marines on Charlie team looked around at each other. Marsden couldn't read minds, but he assumed they were remembering those same words coming from Dollarhyde when they'd found the first alien body.

"Tell us what you're talking about," Dollarhyde said. "And give us a status update on your team. All we know is what your life sign readings are through the PDMs."

"Then I'm sure you've already seen that Popkess is dead," Arizona said. "The rest of us found a room that seems to have an airtight door, but we're still not sure if they might use any kind of service tunnels or vents to get in, so we're remaining on high alert. Graznow lost a leg, and she doesn't look like she's going to make it. Jesus, Dollarhyde. Those things just swarmed up her leg and then, well, it was just gone except for the skeleton. We had to chop that part off before they could swarm up her any farther."

"What do you mean?" Dollarhyde asked. "Give us better details so we know what we're up against."

"Shiltz found a spot that looked like it might have once had one of those blue bubbles, except now the bubble was completely gone. All around it there were little protrusions coming out of the wall and floor, like those barnacle things you used to see on sailing ships back on Earth. They didn't do anything until Schiltz got closer. It was like, I don't know, like they sensed his presence and it woke them up."

Arizona stopped to take a breath and run a hand through her hair. "They're like insects, or maybe crabs, some kind of crustaceans. Each one's probably about as wide as the length of my thumb, but there were hundreds of them. And they didn't move like they were separate creatures. It was like they had a hive mind. They all picked a target and just went for it. Their size made it hard to shoot them, but I think maybe we were able to take out a third of them before we locked ourselves in here."

All the PDMs flashed red to indicate another lost marine.

"Graznow?" Dollarhyde asked.

Arizona nodded grimly. "Graznow. We're doing our best to tend to the injuries we have, but Lochner was our medic. She had the most field medicine knowledge of our group."

"Sit tight," Dollarhyde said. "Make sure you transmit all your mapping data to us. Once I'm positive that everyone in my own team is secure, I'll be sending—"

"Dollarhyde!" Mossier said. "I've got multiple moving targets coming from that direction." He indicated the door that they hadn't yet gone through. "Lots of them. And they're small."

"We'll have to get back to you, Arizona," Dollarhyde said. "It looks like your crab creatures have found another food source—us."

August 2, 2147 (Earth Calendar)
1840 Greenwich Mean Time
Location: Alien Spacecraft Command Room,
Bullfinch-2
Marine Heartbeats Detected on Planet: 40

"Mossier, I want to know exactly how many there are, now!" Dollarhyde yelled. "Axel, Zhou, you better have something set up!"

"I've got several thermite cords on a trigger," Axel said, holding up a remote detonator in her hand. "It'll flash fry anything that's too close when it goes off, but if there's too many of them spread out over too large a space, there's no way it will get all of them."

"I can't get an exact count on how many are coming," Mossier said. "They're too small and there's too many. The scanners are having trouble separating them. There's at least a hundred and fifty, but the actual number is probably a hell of a lot more."

"Everyone, get in position!" Dollarhyde said. "Remember that the choke points are the door and the two sets of stairs. Have knives and melee weapons ready in case any of them get up the stairs and into our ranks. Ranged weapons will be useless trying to get one of those things off your fellow marines."

Marsden and Mingo started for a place on the firing line with all the other Recon Marines, but Dollarhyde waived them off. "Not you two. Get back to those controls. If this ship has some kind of defense system we can use to help us, I want it up and running and on our side, and I want it done five minutes ago. Got it?"

"Affirmative!" Marsden and Mingo said at the same time. As much as Marsden wanted to be on the line doing his part to keep the invading swarm from making a meal of his teammates, he had to acknowledge that Dollarhyde was right. Whatever these things were, however they got here, there had to be something inside the ship that they could use to defend against the crab swarm. Axel's thermite cords would be the most effective way to neutralize a large number of small enemies, but anything that got past that would likely just as easily be able to dodge the wild firing bullets from their MH-56s. There had to be another way.

Marsden and Mingo knelt down next to the controls again. "Please tell me your translation program has something it can give us," Marsden said.

"It's still working. It's not so easy as just find what symbol means what word in our language, after all. There's also matters of context, syntactic structure, and other linguistic considerations."

"Can you at least give me an estimate?" Marsden asked.

Mingo looked at his PDM and shrugged. "If it continues at this rate, we'll maybe get the first portions of a translation in three to four minutes, but I have no way of telling you how complete that translation might be."

Marsden swore and took a look at the controls. He had a knack for operating complicated equipment, but this was all so utterly alien that he wouldn't even know where to begin. He supposed he could try just touching things at random to see if anything responded to him, but he was just as likely to do something stupid like activate a ship-wide self-destruct as he was to turn on security measures that would help them.

"Isn't there anything you can do to speed the translation up?" Marsden asked.

"Maybe, but I can't be as certain that the translation would be correct."

"They're almost here!" Mossier said. Marsden turned to look through the door and down the hall where the crab swarm was supposed to appear, but it was too dark down that way for him to see anything. A soft chittering noise slowly grew with each passing second. Along with the noise there was a god-awful smell, something between rancid fish and burnt oil.

"Do it," Marsden said to Mingo. "We don't have any choice but to take the chance."

"Mossier, I'm marking the placement of my thermite cords on your scanner," Axel said as she quickly fiddled with her PDM. "You need to tell me approximately when the middle of the swarm is over the top of them."

"Got it," Mossier said.

"Everyone, you're going to need to turn your heads," Axel said. "Don't look directly down the hall when the thermite goes off, or it will temporarily blind you and you won't be able to shoot for shit."

The sound and smell grew louder. Marsden thought he could hear tiny screeches mixed in with the chittering noises. The sound was also echoing strangely, almost as if…

A sudden thought occurred to him, a simple question that none of them had thought to ask Delta team that could nonetheless possibly change the entire course of the battle that was about to hit them any second now. Marsden quickly pinged Arizona's PDM again. "Arizona! When you found these things, you said some of them were attached to the wall before they came back to life and came at you?"

"Uh, yeah. Why?"

"Does that mean they could crawl on the walls as well as the floor?"

Arizona's response was drowned out as the sound from the hall reached deafening levels. Marsden didn't need to hear the answer though. He already knew, and while several of the other marines around him looked confused as to why this might be important, Axel understood immediately.

"I only have the thermite set up on the floor!" she called out.

At almost the same time, Mossier yelled, "Now! Do it now!"

Axel hit the switch on her remote detonator, but Marsden already knew what was going to happen. If the enemy had been coming at them exclusively over the floor, the thermite would have roasted many of them and made everything that came afterward that much easier. But anything that was on the walls or ceiling would be able to get through relatively unscathed. It also meant that, if they could come at the defending marines over the walls and ceilings, the choke points at the stairs were pretty much useless.

The marines were in absolutely the wrong formation to make an effective attack.

Everyone turned away at the blinding flash in the hall, and all Marsden could hope was that the crab things in the swarm had some kind of eyes that were sensitive to light, and that the flash would help debilitate them, or at least slow them down a little. They had no such luck, however, as the instant they all turned back to look at the door, the tiny chitinous monstrosities came through over the walls in a shiny black tidal wave.

"Fire! Fire!" Dollarhyde screamed. "Don't let them get past the door!"

The air erupted with the sounds of gunfire and the smell of cordite. Bullets hit the area immediately around the door, exploding uncountable numbers of the crab creatures into a sticky, pale blue goo. For every five that were destroyed, one or two got through and rushed up the wall, spreading to the ceiling, the floor, and into every crack and crevice the creatures could find. Whatever hive mind controlled them, it seemed to be smart. It seemed to know that smaller groups and individual crab creatures would be able to slip through the defenses easier. All it needed to do was slowly advance these small numbers to the dais and then, once there, converge on the marines and have their feast.

"Damn it, Mingo, give me something to work with!" Marsden yelled. "Anything!"

"Maybe…" Mingo's eyes frantically went over his readout, searching for anything at all that might be useful. "There!" He pointed one particularly deep depression near the center of the device. "That might be something to do with powering the ship up!"

Marsden wasted no time thrusting his fist into the depression. It did nothing.

"Too many of them are getting through!" Dollarhyde screamed. Marsden looked back to rest of the group to see that several of the crabs had made it as far as the stairs before getting splattered, but any attempt to concentrate on those resulted in even more scurrying over the walls on ceiling. The first crab to make enough headway over the ceiling dropped down onto the shoulder of one marine, and before anyone had time to try to get it off, the crab rushed to the marine's neck and ripped open his jugular with its small but surprisingly sharp mandibles. The marine collapsed to the ground in a shower of blood, but before the crab had time to go for another target, Axel was on top of it with a knife in hand. She stabbed down, punching right through the creature's carapace, pinning it to the already dead body of the marine. She yanked out the knife and seemed to decide that it wouldn't be worth it to grab her rifle again, and instead concentrated on melee attacking any of the crabs that got through.

"I don't understand," Mingo said. "That should have worked. The translation program said there was an eighty-nine percent chance that hole had something to do with powering up the ship."

Marsden suddenly remembered how they had opened the front door of the ship. "Look for a second console that looks exactly like this one. This race must do everything in pairs!"

As Mingo frantically looked at all the consoles, Marsden looked back again to see that a number of the crabs had formed on continued stream going to the opposite wall while a number of others had spread out in a wide pattern on the wall closer to Dollarhyde. The largest number of marines concentrated on the larger stream, but Marsden thought he saw the tactic the creatures were taking. They might have been small and looked insignificant, but it was evidence that their hive mind was smart enough to recognize who was in charge on the marines' side of the fight.

"Axel!" Marsden yelled. "Protect Dollarhyde! They're going to make a go at her!"

Axel looked in that direction and nodded. She sprinted over to Dollarhyde's side just in time to knock several out of the air as they leaped for Charlie team's current commanding officer. Dollarhyde dropped her own rifle in order to pull a knife and defend herself, and another marine nearby did the same.

"Got it!" Mingo said. Marsden looked at him to see the man shove his own fist into a console that looked nearly identical to Marsden's. The lights in the room suddenly turned on, and the entire ship around them hummed with power. The jelly-like surface of the wall near them flickered, revealing itself now as a view or command screen as various alien symbols flashed across it in incomprehensible patterns.

"That's all well and good," Llewellyn said from where she stood, still firing at the concentrated stream of crabs on the far wall. They seemed to be making a dent in the numbers, but the creatures continued to stream from the door. "But it's not going to help us if it doesn't power some kind of defensive measures in here."

"How about it, Mingo?" Marsden asked. "Please tell me your translation program has something to give us."

"Um, that!" Mingo said, hurriedly pointing to the console at the center of all the others. "It's an incomplete translation, but the symbols on it say something about weapons."

"Good enough for me," Marsden said. He ran to the console and saw that it didn't seem to have a corresponding console anywhere else. In fact, while the others had contained divots and holes all over them, this one was not only smaller than the others but only had one indentation on each side. It was also a drastically different pearlescent purple color. If he had to guess, he'd saw this was the alien equivalent of a large red button that no one should ever press.

"Are you sure about this?" Marsden asked in Mingo's direction.

"No!" Mingo responded.

"Marsden, just do it!" Dollarhyde screamed. Seconds later, that scream turned from one of frustration to one of agony, followed by the loud cussing of Axel and several other marines. Marsden didn't turn to see what had happened. He just clenched both of his hands into fists and shoved them into the depressions on either side.

Nothing happened.

"Mingo, damn it!" Marsden yelled.

"I told you I wasn't sure!" Mingo said. "Wait, I'm getting

something else in the translations… that one! Marsden, go to the console two to your right and put your fist in the upper left corner. I'll get the other one. It says something in the vicinity of locking down the area."

Marsden would have asked Mingo if he was sure this time, except he would have bet that the answer would be the same. Instead Marsden ran over and did exactly as he said. Mingo did the same with the other console.

This time something noticeable did in fact happen. The whole room buzzed like it was gathering some kind of energy. The two doors in and out of the room suddenly flashed with a bright blue covering, and all the crabs that had been half in the room and half out were sliced apart. Those crabs that still hadn't made it into the room tried to stop and turn, but their large numbers and momentum sent them skidding in the doorway and popping apart like popcorn. It was a force field, Marsden realized. No species was supposed to have that kind of technology, yet whoever these aliens were, they'd developed it. Marsden wasn't going to complain, and neither was he going to take a moment to celebrate as all the crabs outside the room screeched in their death throes. They still had all the creatures inside the room to deal with.

Marsden and Mingo turned away from the consoles. Marsden noticed that the force fields stayed on, and they would likely have to find a way to turn them off before they had any hope of getting out of this place, but that was a problem for later. Marsden grabbed one of his side-arms from its holster and started to pick off individual crab monsters that were still heading in Dollarhyde's direction, although Dollarhyde already looked like she was in bad shape. A couple of the creatures must have gotten to her face, because the entire left side of her head looked like little more than a bloody smear. She was probably blind in that eye, and she was obviously weakened, but she still managed to slash and attack a number of the creatures that came at her. Several others must have decided that Axel was now the primary threat, given that she was currently surrounded by their dead and twitching chitinous bodies, but other than a few minor-looking cuts and scrapes on her hands, she looked perfectly fine.

Marsden shot several of the crabs off the wall, then stopped when he realized the room had once again gone completely silent except for the heavy panting of exhausted marines. He lowered his weapon and surveyed the area. The walls, floor, and ceiling were covered in sharp pieces of crab bodies and dripping spatters of sticky blue blood. A number of the marines were injured, but there didn't seem to be any dead other than the unfortunate man who'd had his throat ripped open. Dollarhyde was in bad shape, and Marsden doubted she would live for long, but otherwise it looked like it was all over.

Marsden felt the adrenaline that had been pumping through him leave his body, and he dropped to his knees, no longer able to even support himself. Many of the other Recon Marines did the same, confident now that they were safe.

For the moment, at least.

August 2, 2147 (Earth Calendar)
1849 Greenwich Mean Time
Location: Alien Spacecraft Command Room, Bullfinch-2
Marine Heart Beats Detected on Planet: 39

"Commin Della tim. Gibbus uh zirrep."

Marsden gently took Dollarhyde's PDM from her. "Dollarhyde, I think you're going to have to let the next in command take over for a moment."

Dollarhyde looked up at him. Even with only one eye now, she still looked no-nonsense and formidable. Actually, she looked like even more of a hard-ass than before. Apparently that was the side effect of having half your face eaten off by alien predators.

"Yuh guddah prublum, Merszen? Um ztil uluv, zo um ztil injurge."

Laughingmoon, who had been assisting Conway in tending to Dollarhyde's injuries, looked thoroughly confused. "Does anyone understand what she's trying to say?

"She said that as long as she's still alive, she's still in charge," Marsden said. "Dollarhyde, if your own team can't understand you while we're standing right next to you, then it's highly doubtful that anyone on Delta team will be able to communicate with you either."

"Medic's orders," Conway said as she pulled a canister of medicated foam from her med kit. "You need to stop and rest. Mingo's going to have to take charge, at least for the moment."

Dollarhyde sighed, an action that caused an ugly bubble of pus and blood to form at the side of her mouth. "Grut. Suh yuh guz uhr gunna zitend bebbeh me. Lerd elp duh furz puhzon huh truz to muk meh jiggen zoop er zum hit luk dad."

Laughingmoon looked at Marsden. "What about that one? Did you understand that?"

Marsden shook his head. "Not a single word."

While Conway squirted out a hefty dollop of the medicated foam and spread it over the ruined portion of Dollarhyde's face in order to prevent infection, as well as hopefully stop any poisons that might have been transmitted through the crabs' bites, Mingo took over their attempts to hail Delta team. "Delta team, do you read? Talk to us."

At first the only reply they got back was static. After a few more seconds, though, they heard something that might have been words.

"What the hell's wrong with these things now?" Llewellyn asked. "They were working fine again just before we were attacked."

"We also didn't have the ships power back on at that point," Axel pointed out. "By turning everything back on, we probably increased whatever interference we originally ran into when we entered the ship."

After several more minutes of trying, they finally were able to adjust the transmission enough that they could understand most of what Delta team was trying to say. All they were getting at the moment was audio, though. The video feed was still too messed up for them to see anything. "Charlie team, can… us now?" Arizona's voice said.

"Somewhat," Mingo said. "How's your team holding up?"

"We haven't seen any action… last time you talked. The life signs we're picking up… guys don't say the same thing, though."

"We lost Tungsten in the fight. Multiple other injuries, including Dollarhyde, who's in pretty bad shape, but you know how she is. She's still got a wicked tongue, even when half that tongue is missing right along with a huge part of her face."

"Yeesh. That does... like Dollarhyde, though. The lights are... now, so I'm assuming you've figured out how... on."

"Sort of," Mingo said. "Our translation program is still running on it. Until it figures out more of the symbols we're seeing in here, it looks like we're trapped. We managed to turn on some kind of energy field that killed most of the crab swarm, but it looks like it will probably do the same thing to us if we can't figure out how to turn it off."

"How certain are... the crab swarm is completely gone?" Arizona asked. "Because if they're taken... we can come to you and wait... out how to get out of there."

"As far as wean see, the crab swarm is totally wiped out," Mingo said. "But if you come for us, proceed with caution. We have no idea if individual crab creatures might still be lurking out there."

"Roger that," Arizona said. "Send us... map data you have, and we'll... our way in your direction."

"Sending now," Mingo said. "Good luck."

Arizona signed off right as there was a minor scuffle between Conway and Dollarhyde. "Yuh trutta inneck muh wuff dat an uhl shuffit up yur uth," Dollarhyde said as she tried to push away a hypodermic needle Conway had in her hand.

"Other than the fact that I think that's probably anatomically impossible, you don't have any choice," Conway said. "Right now your system is in shock. You're not feeling the full level of pain you should from your injuries. Once that hits you, it's going to be excruciating. Also, I'm afraid you might have a heart attack, given your current vitals. If you want any chance at all of not dying on this worthless rock of a planet, you'll let me do my job." Before

Dollarhyde could try warding her off again, Conway rudely shoved the needle into Dollarhyde's arm.

"Uhw! Budge," Dollarhyde said before her remaining eye rolled back in her head and she was out cold. When Dollarhyde's body relaxed, Conway finally sat back and allowed herself a deep breath.

"I tell you, commanding officers are always the worst patients," Conway mumbled.

"So what's next?" Marsden asked. Although his question was directly mostly at Mingo, he made sure that anyone in the room could hear in case they had any ideas.

"Well, I sure as hell think those crab things constituted a threat," Chunda said. "Which means we shouldn't be considering this an exploratory mission anymore. It's an extermination."

"I agree," one of the other marines said. "Shouldn't this be the part where we prepare to wipe out this ship and everything on it?"

"I know what Dollarhyde would say here, and that's no," Mingo said. "We've neutralized the crab swarm, as far as we know, and we haven't seen any other threats yet."

"The keyword is 'yet,'" Llewellyn said. "We don't know whether those things were local wildlife or if they were already on the ship when it crashed. Either way, where there's one example of hostile fauna, there's probably a lot more."

"Even if there are more threats on the ship, we still can't leave yet," Mingo said. "At this point, a complete sterilization of all hostile organisms, if there are any more on board, would likely require the destruction of the entire ship. Those crab things could still be in any nook or cranny, after all. And before we destroy the ship, we have to get as much data out of it as possible."

"All these points seem pretty moot to me, anyway," Mossier

said. "Unless we want to destroy the ship while we're still on it, the very first thing we need to do is figure out how to get out of this room without becoming a toasty side dish to the fried crab cakes at the door."

"Marsden and I will work on trying to find an off switch for the energy fields," Mingo said. "Axel and Hemingford, you two see what you can do about maybe disabling them by some other means."

"Blow them up. Got it," Axel said.

"Um, preferably not," Mingo said. "It would be nice to be able to turn them on again if something else came for us."

The PDMs erupted with static, followed by Arizona's voice. "...think we might have a problem."

"What is it?" Mingo asked.

"You... those big blue bubble things we..."

"Say again?" Mingo asked.

"...remember those bubbles we saw earlier?"

"Yeah? What about them?" Mingo asked.

"They're gone."

There was a moment of silence in the command room as all the marines exchanged uneasy glances. Finally Mingo asked, "Arizona, what do you mean they're gone?"

"What isn't there to... I say they're gone, I mean they're gone. Just poof. Vanished. Ex-bubbles. Ceased to... for the fjords."

"I have no idea what you said at the end there," Mingo said, "but I think I get the picture. But how could that happen?"

Arizona didn't have an answer. Marsden, however, thought that he did. "The center console."

Mingo turned to look at him. "What do you mean?"

"While we were trying to find some defensive measures

against the crab swarm," Marsden said. "We activated the center console."

"But it didn't do anything," Zhou chimed in.

"I think it did," Axel said.

"So do I," Marsden agreed. "Just because it didn't do anything that we could see didn't mean it didn't do anything at all."

"So you're saying we somehow mistranslated the symbols on the center console?" Mingo asked. "It destroyed those bubbles instead of activating some kind of weapon?"

Marsden waited for a moment, hoping Mingo would see it without Marsden having to tell him. Finally a look of horror dawned on Mingo's face.

"Oh," he simply said.

"What?" Llewellyn asked. "What am I missing here?"

Axel answered. "When Delta team first found the crab swarm, they were hibernating or sleeping or whatever it was they did in a place where one of the bubbles used to be. They're obviously what killed the crew of this ship, but then they ended up back there, like they treated the area as though it were their home. Then Marsden hit a trigger that supposedly unleashed some kind of weapon, and now all the rest of the bubbles are gone. I don't see how you could possibly need me to keep spelling it out."

"Are you saying there's now a whole hell of a lot more of those crab things running loose all over the ship?" Mossier asked.

"Maybe," Marsden said. "But I don't think so. Delta team saw one large shadow inside that one bubble. I don't think that was another crab swarm. I think that was something else."

"We released some kind of weapon loose on the ship," Mingo said. "Is that what you're trying to say?"

"No. Arizona said there were something like fifty of those

bubbles in that room," Marsden said. "And if two of those bubbles have different kinds of living, biological weapons inside, then all of the others…"

Mingo didn't let him finish. Instead he was back on the PDMs trying to contact Delta team. "Delta team, get out of there now! Proceed to our location immediately. You are in danger!"

The only response he got from Delta team was static, followed by all of Charlie team's PDMs pinging at the death of more marines.

August 2, 2147 (Earth Calendar)
1921 Greenwich Mean Time
Location: Alien Spacecraft Command Room, Bullfinch-2
Marine Heart Beats Detected on Planet: 36

"There goes another one," Conway said grimly as she read the latest data coming through the PDMs. "Lochner. Either she succumbed to her earlier wounds, or something got her."
Charlie team had been sitting her for almost fifteen minutes after completely losing contact with Delta team. Everyone nodded at Conway's announcement. Although the loss of any Recon Marine at all was terrible, Marsden and some of the others took heart that, whatever was happening, only three more marines had died. Whatever hellish things Delta team was facing right now, apparently they were giving them hell right back.

Marsden swore from his place next to the console he'd used to activate the force field. He'd discovered some kind of maintenance access panel early on, but even after he'd figured out how to open it he still couldn't make any sense of the vein and artery-like cords inside. Whoever these aliens were, their technology was completely beyond him or anyone else there. He'd hoped to find some wire he could unplug to disable to fields. There didn't seem to be any plugs, however, or even anything at all that was even slightly recognizable.

Mingo had continued working on the translations this whole time, while Axel thought she had identified some kind of power junction near the doors that she could blow up if they had no other choice. That would get them out of this room, but they all agreed that, while the force fields may be keeping them trapped in here for the time being, they were also protecting them from whatever else might have come from those bubbles.

"Still nothing?" Laughingmoon asked Marsden.

"Nothing would probably be better," Marsden said. "Instead what I am finding in here is a headache. Seriously, whatever this stuff is that they're using to power their technology, it smells worse than Bayne."

Laughingmoon raised an eyebrow. "Not possible."

"If you don't believe me, then get down here, stick your head through that panel, and take a big, deep whiff."

"On second thought, I'll take your word for it," Laughingmoon said.

"That's probably for the best." Marsden sat up and looked over at Mingo. He'd been about to ask Mingo how the translation on the controls was going, but Mingo's attention was now on the jelly-like screen in front of the consoles. "See something interesting, Mingo?"

"Maybe," Mingo said. The screen had turned on right along with everything else when they'd restored power, but no one had paid much attention to it up to this point. They'd been too busy fighting for their lives, licking their wounds, and then trying to find a way out of this place. Now, however, Marsden let the screen grab his attention. The symbols that had appeared there didn't seem to have changed for the last ten minutes.

"Tell me what you're thinking," Marsden asked as he stood up and went to stand next to Mingo.

"I'm thinking I've been going about this the wrong way," Mingo said. "I've been putting all my effort into translating the symbols on the consoles. But the way the translator program works, the more of a language it has to process, the quicker it can go."

"That seems kind of counterintuitive," one of the marines said.

"It might if you don't know much about alien linguistics," Mingo said. "But that's still how it works. We've been sitting here trying to figure out what the markings on the controls mean so that we can find the off switch for the force fields. But maybe what we should be doing is putting the translator program to work on that first." He pointed at the screen. "Once it has all that data processed, it should theoretically have an easier time with the markings on the controls."

"I guess that makes sense," Marsden said. "Also, I'm sure it won't hurt to know what all that stuff on the screen actually says."

Mingo got to work on that, but he wasn't at it for very long before they heard something coming down one of the halls just beyond the force fields. Immediately, every marine that wasn't otherwise occupied got their weapons ready. Even though the field should still be able to hold back any threat, they didn't want to take any chances.

"Wait, hold off," Marsden said after a moment. "I think that's our own people."

Mossier looked down the hall, but the force field caused enough visual distortion that none of them could see very far. "How can you tell?"

"What, you can't smell that?" Marsden asked. "There's only one thing in the galaxy that smells that foul, and it's not any kind of alien."

"I heard that!" Bayne called from somewhere down the corridor. Charlie team collectively made a sigh of relief, but that moment of feeling safe only lasted as long as it took for Bayne and the others to reach the force field. Up close, Marsden could now easily see that Bayne's group was significantly smaller than it had any right to be. Marsden quickly did the arithmetic in his head.

"Bayne, where are the other ten members of Delta team?" Marsden asked.

Trieloff, one of the three other marines that had come down the corridor with Bayne, shook his head. "We have no idea. We were hoping they'd already made it to you guys."

"Well, they're certainly not dead," Conway said. "The PDMs would have told us if they were."

"But that doesn't necessarily mean they're safe, either," Marsden said. "Talk to us, Trieloff. What happened? The last any of us were able to communicate with Delta team, you were all in that room that used to have the blue bubbles."

Trieloff shook his head. "I wish I could tell you, but it happened way too fast for any of us to see. We were able to hear some of what your team was talking about, but then all of a sudden the audio feeds on our PDMs went completely dead. There was a smell, a sort of skunk-like stench in the air, and then, well, something just came at us."

"What came at you?" Axel asked.

"Whatever it was, it was something big," Bayne said. "Taller than me, I think. And maybe it was hairy, too."

"Big and hairy," Llewellyn said in a nonplussed tone. "Very helpful description."

"Yeah, and that's about all the description you're going to get from us for now, too," Trieloff said. "Because it was also fast. We just saw this huge blur of hair coming at us, and before anyone could even aim their MH-56s, this thing took out Huang."

"Took him out how?" Marsden asked.

"Um, it rolled over him," Bayne said.

"Wait, what?" Llewellyn asked.

Trieloff shrugged. "I guess that's about as good a way to describe what happened as anything. It was like a giant furry buzz saw flew through the room. It hit Huang right in the middle and, well, he kind of exploded. His torso and head were just gone, turned into, like, a meat shower."

Llewellyn paled. "That's a rather disturbing visual."

"All that was left afterward were his arms and legs," Bayne said. "I was standing right near him, and I got his elbow right in the face."

"Huang was between us four and the others," Trieloff said. "We immediately ducked for cover down a side corridor, but in the process we got cut off from the others."

"This, uh, fur-coated razor blade thing?" Marsden asked. "Was that the only thing you saw? Or did you happen to see anything else."

"No, we didn't," Trieloff said. "And honestly, if Hairy and the crab swarm are any indication of what else might have been in those bubbles, it's probably an awfully good thing we didn't run into anything else. Because then there probably wouldn't even be four of us standing here."

"Yeah, about that," Mingo said from where he'd stood in front of the screen at the other side of the room. "I think I might have a better clue about what we're dealing with."

Marsden left the group at the force field to join Mingo. "Have you finished the translation of the screen?"

"Enough to understand the context of what it's saying. Once we have a full translation we might be able to use the consoles to bring up further information, but for now it appears to be a list of the commands we executed when we used the consoles." Mingo pointed at the translation on his PDM, then back up at the screen. "See? This first bit here is acknowledging that we turned the power back on to the whole ship. This part at the end confirms that we activated the emergency command room lockdown protocols."

"What about that huge block of symbols in between them?" Marsden asked.

"That's the interesting and disturbing part," Mingo said. "That whole section corresponds to when you activated the center console."

"The weapons?" Marsden asked.

Mingo nodded. "Yes. We just didn't understand the context of what those weapons were or what they were supposed to be for. Each one of these groups of symbols refers to the shutting down of one specific 'cage,' as in the blue bubbles."

"Does it give any specifics about what was in each cage?" Marsden asked. "Or why they were there in the first place?"

"I'm still working on that," Mingo said, "but judging from what I'm seeing, those cages were the whole reason this ship existed."

"So, what, this ship is some kind of ark?" Zhou asked.

"I'll be able to say more once I dig deeper into all this," Mingo said. "I think maybe we have enough of a translation now that I can figure out how to access more data, which I should be able to scan into our PDMs right away and then translate as we go along."

"That's all well and good, but have you figured out how to turn off the force fields yet?" Marsden asked.

"Give me a few more minutes and yeah, I think maybe I can."

"Can you try to maybe go faster than that?" Bayne said through the force field. "I'm not exactly thrilled about being on this side of the protective barrier."

Marsden raised an eyebrow. "Bayne, is there ever anything

you're thrilled about?"

"No," Bayne said grouchily, then looked in Axel's direction. "Well, maybe sometimes."

Everyone in the room took note of the way he looked at Axel except Axel herself. She was too busy fidgeting with a grenade in her hand, pulling the pin out and then putting it back in over and over.

"Uh, Axel? Could you please not do that?" Chunda asked.

Axel looked confused. "Why?"

"Chunda, forget it," Marsden said. "All she's going to do is rattle off some calculation about how unlikely the odds are that she's going to blow us all up."

"3217 to one," Axel said.

The PDMs lit up with an incoming transmission. Marsden had to do a double take at his when he saw that they were once again broadcasting by an audio and a video feed.

"Charlie team, this is Delta team. Come in." The face that appeared on the video belonged to Murakame, but just at a glance Marsden immediately felt like something was wrong.

"Murakame?" Mingo said. "Give us a status report on the rest of your team."

"We are fine," she said. She said the words with almost no inflection, as if she were just reading from a script. "You need to come to us."

Mingo looked at Marsden, then the others. Every single person in the room had an uneasy look on their face. Conway took over the feed from Mingo. "Murakame, are you okay? We were told you were one of the ones who was severely injured in the crab swarm attack."

Murakame paused. Her face showed a complete lack of emotion. "I am fine. It is important that you come to us. You must do it now."

"Who's us?" Conway asked. "Are all the remaining members of Delta team with you?"

A thought suddenly occurred to Marsden. He gestured to get Conway's attention, then pointed at the four members of Delta team waiting just beyond the force field. For a second it looked like Conway didn't understand what he was trying to say. Marsden gestured again, and Conway finally seemed to get it.

"Yes, everyone is here," Murakame said. "We are fine."

Conway looked like she was thinking for a second. "What about Bayne. Is he with you? Axel really wants to know. You know how she feels about him."

Axel cocked her head curiously at Conway, but Marsden waved Axel off, trying to make sure she didn't say anything to give away Conway's lie.

"Bayne is here with us," Murakame said. "He is fine. All of you must come to us."

After a few seconds of hesitation, Conway cut off the feed.

"Everyone, disable the video and audio feeds on your PDMs," Marsden said. "We don't want anything we do or say to get back to her. Or them. Or whoever the hell that really was. Because I can tell you one thing for certain: that wasn't Murakame."

August 2, 2147 (Earth Calendar)
1937 Greenwich Mean Time
Location: Alien Spacecraft Command Room,
Bullfinch-2
Marine Heartbeats Detected on Planet: 36

"I think I've finally got it," Mingo said from the consoles. "Hemingford, you look like you're not doing anything but picking your ass. Get over here and help me with this."

While Hemingford went over to help disable the force fields, Llewellyn paced impatiently at the base of one of the stairs. "Okay, I'm still not getting it. If you don't think that was Murakame that we saw on the PDM, then just who the hell do you think it was?"

"How would I know?" Marsden said. "But she said Bayne was with them, and obviously he's not. And she didn't even bat an eyelash when Conway said that Axel felt something for him, when every single one of us knows that Axel is completely clueless about Bayne."

Axel did in fact look confused. "I have no idea what you're talking about."

Bayne cursed from beyond the force field. "You're killing me over here, Axel."

Axel cocked her head. "You look perfectly alive and healthy to me."

"We have no idea what sort of creatures might have been in those bubble cages," Marsden said. "For all we know, there might have been some kind of shape shifter that was pretending to be Murakame."

"Murakame's still alive, though," Conway said. "The PDMs

would have told us if she were dead." As if to confirm this, she glanced down at her own PDM again. Whatever she saw there made her frown.

"What is it?" Marsden asked.

"It says that Murakame is still alive, but the life signs I'm picking up from her are weird. Irregular heartbeat, low blood-pressure, and her brainwave activity—well, I don't even have the slightest clue how to characterize that. It's all over the place. She may not be dead, but her body is under significant distress."

"It couldn't just be from her earlier injuries?" Marsden asked.

"Some of those symptoms, maybe. But not all of them. And she's not the only one showing bodily distress."

"Who else?" Marsden asked.

Conway paled. "It looks like all of them. Every member of Delta team who isn't currently here with us seems to be in some kind of danger."

As Marsden cursed, Mingo came over to him. "I think we're all done here. I know which controls to use to deactivate the force fields, and I've saved as much data from the ship that I possibly can in such a short period of time. If we weren't fighting for our lives at this point, there would probably be a treasure trove of information we could get from the ship."

"So what's the plan instead?" Llewellyn asked.

Mingo stood straighter and got a grim look on his face. "We go back to our original mission parameters. Clearly, the life we've found on the ship is hostile. Our first and foremost job now is to eliminate all threats."

"Is that such a good idea?" Marsden asked. "Our numbers are already depleted, and just from two threats. If every single one of those bubbles had some kind of deadly creature in it, then I don't see how we can possibly sterilize the whole ship."

"Really?" Axel asked as she fingers a wad of plastic explosives she had pulled from a pouch. She was absent mindedly rolling it into the shape of a grenade. "Because I see how we can do it quite easily."

"If you're suggesting we just blow up the ship and everything on it, that would be counter to why we were sent here to begin with," Conway said. "The first objective was to secure the site so that the Science Corps could come in and do their thing with it."

"Since I'm currently the highest conscious member in the chain of command, the decision falls to me," Mingo said. "And as much as we could learn from this ship and the creatures on it, I'm going to go with Axel on this one. Look at what Hairy and the crab swarm did to two teams of highly trained Recon Marines. If anything from this ship were to get off this planet and back to a human-inhabited world, the results would be devastating. We can't run the risk. The data we managed to pull from the ship is going to satisfy the Science Corps for now."

"Fine. I'm outvoted, not that I really had a vote anyway," Conway said. "But that leaves the question of how we're going to destroy the ship. One or two well placed explosive charges aren't going to be enough to destroy the entire ship along with everything on it."

"No, but hopefully we can find some key weak points in the data we've collected," Mingo said. "As we're on our way, I'll have several of you marines combing through the translations as they come through. Look for anything that A, would help us take out any threats that we come across, and B, will give us some way to eliminate the entire ship."

"And in the mean time?" Marsden asked.

"Isn't it obvious?" Mingo said. "We're Recon Marines. We don't leave our own behind if there's still any chance at all that they could live. We're going to go find the rest of Delta team and get them out of here."

They had the force fields down shortly after that. Bayne, Trieloff, and the other two from Delta team joined them in the command room, where they all made sure they were properly reloaded and ready to go. Dollarhyde at this point was conscious again, but she was still in no shape to walk. Conway rigged up a makeshift stretcher and then lashed the stretcher with Dollarhyde on it to Bayne's heavy ammo packs. He was the one most likely to be able to pull her without tiring. Once they were all ready, Mingo took the lead down the hall from which Bayne and the others had come from. Marsden poured over the still-translating data as they walked.

"It looks like we've got something to call our mysterious alien race that ran this ship," Marsden said. "If this translation is correct, then they literally call themselves something to the effect of 'The Stenani, but better.'"

"That could be a mouthful," Mossier said. "Especially if we're trying to curse their names and their grandmothers while we're in the middle of battle."

"Call them the Sten-Plus, then," Marsden said. "I'm not seeing any specifics about their origins or their relation to the Stenani, but the translation program is listing a long list of very rude words they apparently call their non-Plus brethren. I guess there's no love lost between the two races, if they really are two separate races at all."

"All of that is well and good," Mingo said, "but considering all of the Sten-Plus on this ship appear to be dead, I'm not too worried about them quite yet."

"Not yet, no, but a lot of this information looks very worrying," Marsden said.

"Worrying in what way?" Conway asked. Marsden held up a hand for her to give him a moment as he read the data scrolling across his PDM. They continued to slink carefully down the corridor as he did, with everyone very careful to check corners and listen for any incoming threat.

"Okay," Marsden finally said. "If the translation is right, and I don't see any reason to doubt that it is at this point, it's very important that someone among us survives and makes it back to Command."

"That sounds like an omelet," Bayne said.

"Wait, it sounds like what?" Chunda asked him.

"An omelet. You know, that thing where it sounds like something bad is about to happen."

They all paused as they tried to translate what Bayne was trying to say. Apparently he could sometimes be tougher to understand than the previously unknown alien language currently decoding itself on their PDMs.

"Uh, I think he means it sounds ominous," Marsden said. "And yes, it is."

"Don't leave us in suspense, Marsden," Mingo said.

"Wait, does anybody smell something?" Zhou asked.

"Seriously guys, just stop it," Bayne said. "I know I don't smell like violets, but I don't smell as bad as..." He sniffed the air. "I don't smell as bad as that."

"Smells like a skunk," Zhou said.

After a second to process that, Mingo screamed. "Everyone, take cover! Defensive..."

Something moved down the corridor ahead of them with a flash of speed that turned it into little more than a blur. Most of the marines managed to jump to either side of the corridor in time, leaving an open path down the center, and Dollarhyde protested incoherently as her stretcher was upended in the process. The only two who didn't manage to get out of the way in time were Mingo and Zhou.

Marsden hadn't known what to think of Bayne's and Trieloff's description of the creature when they had first mentioned it, but with the brief glimpse he got in those first few seconds, Marsden realized there couldn't have possibly been any other way to describe it. It was tall. It seemed to be hairy. And whatever it did to Mingo and Zhou, it accomplished it with a brutal, bloody efficiency that Marsden would have never thought possible from a living creature. The thing hit Mingo head on, and the impression Marsden got was that Mingo was ripped neatly in half. Zhou wasn't in exactly the middle of the hallway, so he fared slightly better. Everything from his left shoulder down exploded in a gory mess that splattered all the other marines. Unable to support himself as the creature vanished down the corridor behind them, Zhou fell over to his side, causing several unidentifiable organs to leak out through the massive gaping wound.

They were all still for several seconds before the situation caught up to them. Most of the marines quickly turned around in the direction the hairy creature had gone, all of them training their weapons that way and keeping a tight hold on the triggers in case the thing suddenly came back. The smell had subsided, so Marsden didn't think it was coming back this way.

Conway was the only one who rushed to get back into the middle of the corridor. She took a quick glance at the remains of Mingo and, with the calm that only a combat medic ever seemed to possess, immediately dismissed Mingo as a complete lost cause. Zhou, on the other hand, still appeared to be breathing. Marsden joined her, taking Conway's med kit from her and preparing to hand her anything she needed.

"If Zhou's going to have any chance of surviving at all," Conway said, "then the first thing we need to do is cauterize the wound."

Marsden looked down at the gaping mass of gore where Zhou's left arm, leg, and parts of his rib cage were missing, and he immediately knew that there really wasn't any chance for Zhou to live at all. Not that he was going to tell Conway that. He'd learned in the past that there was no way to stop a Recon Marines combat medic from tending to someone if they believed there was even the slightest chance the victim could live. Rather than try to stop her and get her to conserve their medical supplies, it was best to just let Conway do her thing.

"Hand me the CV5 canister," Conway said to Marsden. He quickly rooted through her pack and found the can of medicated gel. It was similar to what she had used on Dollarhyde, as far as Marsden's limited combat medicine knowledge could tell him, but it was for far more extreme situations like amputations.

Zhou's eyes rolled back in his head and he looked like he was trying to say something, but before he could he spit up a gout of dark blood. Before Conway deployed the med gel, Zhou's chest stopped moving and a last few bubbles of bloody spittle came out of the side of his mouth with his death rattle.

"Conway, stop," Marsden said.

"No, I can still…" Conway paused, as though seeing the severity of the ruined man before her for the first time. All of their PDMs had already declared Zhou dead. She was simply the last one to acknowledge it.

August 2, 2147 (Earth Calendar)
1956 Greenwich Mean Time
Location: Corridor of Sten-Plus Spacecraft, Bullfinch-2
Marine Heartbeats Detected on Planet: 34

"We need to get out of this main hallway," Marsden said. With Mingo dead, that made him the highest ranking marine here except for Dollarhyde, who was still too out of it at the moment to give commands, and Arizona, wherever she might be. "Hairy might come back."

"Are you sure that's a good idea?" Llewellyn asked. "So far we don't have any map data on anything other than the two main corridors, and so far the layout of this place doesn't exactly look intuitive."

"No, I'm not sure at all," Marsden said. "But I do know that Hairy has managed to take out three of us so far without anyone even being able to get a shot off at it. Judging from its size, it shouldn't be able to travel as quickly down smaller corridors. Or at least I hope."

Essentia, a younger recruit who had taken over going over the translation data now that Mingo was gone and Marsden was busy trying to keep them all alive, chimed in. "It looks like the information the Sten-Plus had on that creature supports that idea," she said. "There's a note in its file that, in the event that it were to escape on the ship, tighter corridors were the best way to defend against it. Apparently it can fit, but it doesn't like being slowed down."

"That's good to know," Marsden said as he led all them down the nearest side hallway. "Is there anything else in there that would be able to help us?"

"Loads," Essentia said. "Too much of it for me to just rattle off right now."

"Keep digging through it," Marsden said. "Any tiny detail could be the difference between life and death."

As they cautiously proceeded down the new corridor, Conway asked, "Do we even know where we're trying to go? The ten remaining members of Delta team could be anywhere, and if you still want to keep radio silence, it's not exactly like we can ping them and ask them all where they are."

"The only option that I see is to head back in the direction of the bubble cage room," Marsden said. "It's the last place anyone saw them, so it has to be the first place where we look."

"It's also where we're probably going to find a whole bunch of things that want to rip us apart," Bayne said. Marsden simply nodded. Bayne was right, but there was no way around that without considering leaving their fellow marines behind. That wasn't an option.

"Marsden, you started to say something right before Hairy attacked us," Axel said. "Something about how it was important for us to get out of here and warn Command about what we saw here. What were you talking about?"

"While I was going through the translated files, I came across something like—I don't know. It was some kind of manifesto or mission statement for the Sten-Plus regarding the purpose of this ship," Marsden said. "It seems that while humans might not have been aware of the existence of the Sten-Plus before now, they have certainly been aware of us."

"What do you mean?" Mossier asked.

"I mean they've been watching us. Humanity in general, but the Recon Marines in particular. The statement said that whoever was in charge of the Sten-Plus has been watching our skirmishes and interactions with other alien races, especially the Stenani. And they've decided that we're a threat."

"What does that have to do with this ship?" Conway asked.

"The best the translation program could come up with is calling this ship a biological weapons research facility. Top secret, as far as I could tell. It's been going to a wide variety of planets we haven't found yet, and it's been gathering any alien life that the Sten-Plus could use against us in the event that they decide they need to go to war with us. The creatures on this ship were apparently hand selected to be the weapons that would cause humanity the most damage."

"Shit," Laughingmoon said. "So far I would definitely say that their plan is working."

"There were also a few vague references to 'other measures' that the Sten-Plus might be preparing to use against humans," Marsden said. "So yeah, we need to get this information to Command. A lot more lives than just our own are riding on it."

"Marsden, I wasn't kidding when I said there was a lot of data on the creatures that are loose on this ship," Essentia said. "Is there anything specific I should be looking for at first?"

"Yeah," Marsden said. "Specifically look for anything that might explain what we saw earlier with Murakame. Make that your top priority."

"Looks like there's some kind of larger room up ahead," Trieloff said. "It might be a good place for something to try ambushing us."

"Agreed," Marsden said. "Everyone, stay focused and ready."

The room they came to was larger than the command room, yet it didn't appear to be as large as the room with the bubble cages. Like everything else on the ship, this room had a peculiar organic look. In the center of the room, with irregular stairs and catwalks leading all around it, there was a single large structure that appeared to pulse weakly with blue light. Something about the multi-chambered structure of it made Marsden think of a heart, but for some reason there were no lights on in the ceiling like there had been in other rooms, leaving most of the room cast in shadow.

"Correct me if I'm wrong, but this place looks like some kind of power core," Conway said.

"I don't think I will correct you," Marsden said. "Essentia? Anything you can find on this place in the data files."

"Give me a second," she said as she scrolled through the massive amount of data crowding her PDM screen. "Right. Here's a reference to a secondary power room. Or is it a third? Hold on… okay. Three. Apparently there are three power cores that supply power to the entire ship."

"How does that thing even work?" Hemingford asked.

One of the other marines sniffed. "I don't know, but it smells a hell of a lot better than Hairy did. It's almost pleasant. Like flowers."

"Marsden," Axel said. "This would probably be the perfect place to set some charges. It's kind of difficult to tell with the technology we've seen so far, but maybe if we destroyed all three of the power cores at once, that would be enough to destroy the whole ship."

Marsden nodded. "Sounds like a better plan than anything else we've been able to come up with so far. Would you be able to set it up to remote detonate all three cores at the same time?"

"Affirmative. Just let me rig this room, and all we would have to do from there is find the other two."

"Great," Marsden said. "Then we find the rest of our people, get a safe distance from the ship, and blow this entire place sky high. Essentia, see if you can find anything to support the idea that this would work."

Essentia sighed. "I'll try, but you've already got me looking up a gazillion different things all at once."

"Just do your best. Get a few of the others to help you if you need it," Marsden said. As Axel had another marine help her place explosive charges at strategic places around the core, Marsden noticed something strange on the floor just around the other side of the core. "What's that over there?"

Mossier and another marine cautiously approached the objects that Marsden had indicated. They looked like they were the broken remains of three or four calcium-covered spheres, each one about the size of a human head. "Whatever they are, they were hollow," Mossier said. He looked back at Marsden with sudden trepidation. "Do you think something was inside?"

"Like they were eggs or something?" Marsden asked. He really did not like the possibilities there. "Essentia, I hate to be a pain, but..."

"Actually, I think I already saw something about that," Essentia said as she rushed back through the day. "Right here. Occupant of stasis field number eleven. Uh, it's some kind of alien plant or fungus."

Marsden relaxed slightly. "That doesn't sound too bad." Then he tensed again as he remembered that, if it wasn't too bad, it wouldn't have been hidden on a ship full of biological weapons and trapped in a bubble-like stasis field. "If it's a plant, how did it get all the way here from the cage room?"

"Um, the translation is a bit spotty here, but it says something about the plant spores being attracted to energy sources, which help them grow. I guess that, in spore form, they have some kind of limited locomotion?"

"In spore form," Marsden muttered. That would probably be when they were inside those broken spheres. But what would these plant things look like once they were out? "Axel, you're done," he said quietly.

"But I've only placed three charges," Axel said. "For maximum concussive effect, I need to place at least…"

"I said you're done," Marsden said. He looked around the room for any sign of what might have come out of the spores, but given the organic look of the ship, he had no idea what in the room was supposed to be there and what would be out of place. He did, however, see another hall leading out on the far side of the room. "Everyone, be careful and watch your step. Head for that other door. We don't know what…"

He stopped when he saw something slimy and viscous drip from the ceiling nearby Mossier and the other marine.

Slowly, partly because he didn't want to startle anything and partly because he wasn't actually sure he wanted to know what he was about to see, Marsden looked up. All of the other marines followed his gaze to the place in the ceiling where there should have been some kind of lights. He could see now that there *were* lights, except they were faint, like something thick was covering them.

Something thick and moving.

"Quietly," Marsden said. "No sudden movements. Whatever it is, we don't want to…"

Mossier took a step back right onto one of the pieces of calcified sphere. It broke with a loud, sharp cracking noise.

The ceiling came alive with tentacles.

Marsden didn't waste any time. He immediately started firing at the ceiling, not knowing exactly what he needed to aim for but realizing that any damage to the creature might be what saved them. The sinewy tentacles whipped down, each one trying to wrap itself around one of the marines. In those first few seconds Marsden registered that the tentacles seemed to be clumped, although he didn't understand why until three man-sized pods burst open and dripped slime down on them.

"Some kind of carnivorous plants!" Marsden yelled. "Three of them! Aim for the central pods!"

Before he could even finish getting those words out, though, several of the tentacles wrapped around Mossier and the other marine that had been standing next to him. The tentacles yanked them up to the ceiling before anyone on the ground could react. The tentacles shoved both marines into one of the pods, which snapped shut over them. The pod convulsed like it was swallowing, then it opened again to reveal nothing. Marsden though he could see something right next to the pod that looked like a giant bladder that swelled with its two victims, although the bladder immediately started convulsing around its prey as though crushing them. They weren't inside the plant for more than three seconds before everyone's PDMs lit up again with the news that two more marine heart beats had disappeared.

"The tentacles are too fast!" Hemingford said. He started to head in the direction where they'd come in.

"No, not that way!" Marsden said. "Hairy's still out there! We have to go through the other door."

As if they were able to hear and understand, the plant on the ceiling closest to that door dropped several of its tentacles to form a loose curtain over their escape route.

"It doesn't look like we're going to be able to get out that way," Hemingford said.

Before Marsden could think of the best plan of attack, Axel

shouldered her rifle and instead pulled out a long, wicked-looking knife with one hand and a grenade with the other. "I'm on it!" she said. "Cover me!"

"Axel, don't!" Conway yelled at her. "You're going to—" A tentacle lashed out at Conway, who ducked and rolled out of the just in time to avoid it wrapping around her.

"You heard the woman, everyone! Cover her!" Marsden said. The marines grouped into a spread-out formation. Rather than taking a defensive posture, though, Axel ran right for the tentacles hanging in front of the door. She didn't even try to avoid them as one wrapped around her waist and yanked her off the floor.

"Oh hell, no you don't!" Bayne said as he shifted his heavy machine gun into place.

"Wait, I know what she's doing!" Marsden said. "Don't try to make that tentacle drop her. Instead concentrate your fire on all the other tentacles. Don't let them get too tight of a grip on her."

"Uh, I know everyone loves Axel," Laughingmoon said, "but maybe we should also make sure none of the tentacles get us either?"

Bayne and Marsden concentrated their fire on the other tentacles coming from the plant that blocked the door, while everyone else worked on fending off the other two plants. While their bullets worked quite well in ripping through the tentacles when they hit, the tentacles were fast enough to dodge them in most cases. Every attempt to shoot directly at the pods seemed to fail. Whatever vegetable material covered the actual pods, it appeared to be too thick for the bullets to get very far in and cause any real damage.

The tentacle that had grabbed Axel probably would have been quick enough to pop her into its mouth if she hadn't been armed, but Axel was a whirling buzz saw with her knife. Despite her precarious and dangerous situation, Marsden could see the cold calculation in her eyes as she very intentionally aimed each stab into the tentacle with her knife, as if she were figuring out exactly which weak spots to hit to slow it down yet not cause it to drop her. It continued to pull her up and up, closer to its waiting maw, and yet Axel didn't at all seem like it concerned her.

"Axel!" Bayne screamed, his voice barely audible over the constant roar of his chain gun. "I swear, if you let yourself die to that stupid thing, I'll kill you!"

The closer Axel got to the open pod, the less she struggled. If Marsden didn't know any better he would have said she looked like she was giving up the fight, but he knew her far better than that. With only centimeters between her and the pod, Axel did something improbably and amazing. She made one final slash with her knife at the tentacle that held her, and only know did Marsden see how truly calculated all her other attacks had been. This final slash severed something vital in the tentacle, and it went completely limp, falling away from her. Yet she didn't try to escape. Instead, she did the exact opposite. She used her knife to hold herself up on the tentacle, then actually thrust herself up directly into the open pod. Marsden saw something fall from her, and it wasn't until later that he realized what it was. It was a grenade pin.

Flipping herself upside down, Axel hit the inner flesh of the open pod with her feet and then immediately kicked out, hurtling herself away. Feeling that its prey was exactly where it wanted her to be, the jaws of the pod snapped shut, barely missing Axel as she fell away. She grabbed onto the dead tentacle for a moment to break her fall slightly, and Marsden noticed that she did it with one hand still on her knife and the other empty. The grenade was gone.

She slid down the tentacle for a short moment, then dropped the rest of the down the floor and rolled with the impact. "Duck and cover!" she yelled at the other marines.

The pod over the door exploded with a loud *hrumpf* noise, showering the marines in dark green vegetable matter and light green slime. In its death throes the carnivorous plant even seemed to give off one final burst of floral scent, a strangely pleasant sensation among all the gunfire and shouting. The tentacles that had been blocking the door suddenly went limp, and a path opened for them.

"Move!" Marsden said. "Everyone out of the room!"

The two remaining pods did their best to reach for the marines on their way out, but Marsden and Bayne stayed back the longest, continually firing so their bullets chewed their way through the tentacles. Bayne was the last one out, and he collapsed on the floor where everyone else rested to catch their breath.

"That is why I will never, ever be a vegetarian," Bayne said. "I refuse to eat anything that might try to eat me back."

Marsden was too exhausted to tell Bayne that he was an idiot.

August 2, 2147 (Earth Calendar)
2008 Greenwich Mean Time
Location: Corridor of Sten-Plus Spacecraft, Outside of Power Core Room Three, Bullfinch-2
Marine Heartbeats Detected on Planet: 32

They all took a precious moment to rest just outside the power core room. Dollarhyde was awake enough now that she complained that she didn't get any action against the three carnivorous plants, but for everyone else the adrenaline had finally caught up to them and they needed to take a breather. Marsden made sure they were far enough away from the door that none of the tentacles would be able to reach through, but he still kept Bayne and several others guarding the door. As plants, the two remaining pods shouldn't be able to move and come after them, but they couldn't afford to make any assumptions regarding the flora and fauna loose on the ship.

Marsden did a quick check of all the remaining Recon Marines under his command. "Any injuries?"

"I think we're all fine," one of the marines said, which prompted Llewellyn to shoot him a dirty look.

"I'm pretty sure Mossier would disagree," she said. She hid her emotions well, but Marsden thought he caught a small hitch in her voice. He remembered a rumor that Llewellyn and Mossier had been an item at one point, but he wasn't going to question her on it. She had every right to mourn any marine that might have been her friend or lover, but those moments of pain and grief needed to hold off as much as possible until everyone that remained was once again safe on the *Franklin Dixon*.

"Axel, what about you?" Marsden asked. He noticed that, at

his question, Bayne was suddenly paying a lot more attention to the conversation. Axel, as always, completely missed Bayne's interest.

"I'm alright," Axel said. "Nothing like almost being eaten by a giant carnivorous plant to remind you that you're truly alive."

Llewellyn choked at that comment and looked away. Again, Axel seemed oblivious to the effect her words had on those around her. When this was all over, Marsden might try to have a word with her about paying more attention to what was going on around her, although he didn't think it would make much of a difference.

"What about the charges you set?" Marsden asked. "Is three going to be enough to blow the core?"

"We have no way of knowing for sure," Axel said. "For all we know, twenty charges might not be enough to even put a dent in that thing. Or flicking a match at it might cause the entire ship to go nuclear. We're just playing guessing games at this point."

Laughingmoon spoke up. "Shouldn't we be worried that the two remaining pods might try to disable the charges? Or maybe even eat them?"

"Yes, we could do that," Axel said. "Or we could actually worry about things we can control."

"Hopefully those pods have at least enough sentience or intelligence to realize that if they try it, they might end up like their friend," Marsden said.

"Or the charges might just be too small to catch the plants' attention," Axel said. "I'd give percentages on those possibilities, but my data set in this situation is woefully incomplete."

"Everyone should take five minutes to find a corner to relieve themselves in or eat some of their rations," Dollarhyde said groggily from her stretcher. "We can't afford any distractions."

"Glad to have you back with us for the moment," Marsden said. "And I'm also glad we can actually understand what you're saying again."

"Probably has something to do with this foam crap all over my face. Could someone please let me out of these straps?"

"I'm not sure that you're in any position to walk by yourself just yet," Conway told her.

"I need to piss," Dollarhyde said. "Either you let me out of these straps so I can go about my business, or else you're the one who's going to have to clean up after me, Conway."

Conway promptly released Dollarhyde from the stretcher.

Marsden took a moment to sit and pulled out a ration to munch on. Essentia was right next to him, and Marsden offered her a bite.

"I already had one of my own," Essentia said. She wouldn't look at Marsden, instead keeping all her attention on her PDM and the flow of data passing over the screen. There was a distinct quaver in her words that Marsden thought he recognized.

"How many missions is this for you, marine?" he asked her.

"Two," Essentia said quietly.

"And I'm betting your first one wasn't anything like this?" Marsden asked. Despite herself, Essentia smiled.

"I've already been warned not to make bets with you."

"It's a figure of speech. You know what I mean."

Essentia nodded. "My first mission was a security detail for an ambassador from Io. There were a few minor skirmishes involved."

"But nothing even close to this," Marsden said.

"No. Not even a little."

"You look scared."

"I'm a Recon Marine, Marsden. Just because I'm green

doesn't mean I'm going to let it affect my duty here. You don't need to worry about me."

Marsden nodded, satisfied with her answer, then gestured at her PDM. "Have you been able to find anything else in there that might be useful to us?"

Before she could answer, all their PDMs pinged with an incoming signal. They were switched off from directly receiving or sending anything from the missing marines, but the PDMs could still pick up any signals that Murakame or anyone else might try to send.

"That's not a message being sent to us," Marsden said.

"Who the hell else would Murakame being trying to contact?" Hemingford asked.

Marsden shrugged, then pulled out his own PDM and adjusted it so that he could listen in on the transmission. It was indeed possible for Murakame to send a more secure message that Charlie team wouldn't be able to listen in on, so either whatever was pretending to be Murakame didn't know that, or else she didn't care who heard it.

"*Franklin Dixon*, come in," Murakame said. Although her tone still sounded vaguely off, it wasn't quite as inflectionless as it had been the first time. Another picture appeared on the PDMs next to her as del Mar, one of the marines who had remained behind on the *Franklin Dixon*, responded.

"Murakame? We've been trying to reach anyone from either of the two teams for almost an hour," del Mar said. "Give us an update. All we're seeing so far is heavy casualties. Are you okay?"

"I am not fine," Murakame said. "We need Dropship Beta sent down immediately."

"What's gone wrong?" del Mar asked. "Our instruments say

that Dropship Alpha is still in working condition."

"Dropship Alpha has been invaded. There are some kind of parasites on board the alien ship. They have taken over all of Charlie team and some of Delta team. There are only three of us left."

"Son of bitch," Marsden muttered. He already had a good idea what del Mar would ask next, right along with Murakame's reply. He would have thought it was a little bit genius if it wasn't about to cause some serious problems. "We have to interrupt Murakame's broadcast. Now. Or at least send our own message to the Dixon."

Before anyone could do any such thing, del Mar asked, "What do you mean? We're still reading life signs for thirty-two separate marines on the planet."

Dollarhyde cursed as she hit her PDM. "I'm trying to get through to the *Dixon*, but it's like we're being jammed. Whatever it is Murakame's doing to get through to the *Dixon* without any interference, she must also be doing something to keep us from joining in."

"We are the only ones that are left," Murakame said. "Everyone else has been taken over by parasites. We need to get back to the *Franklin Dixon* immediately so we can report what we have found."

Although del Mar still looked confused, he nodded grimly. "Understood. We'll immediately send Dropship Beta down with everyone we can spare to help you."

Murakame paused. "Negative."

Now del Mar really looked perplexed. "Say again, Murakame?"

She was quicker this time. "Negative. Do not send down any more marines. We need to insure that we do expose anyone else to the possibility of these parasites."

Marsden silently cheered as del Mar finally went from mere not understanding what was going on to straight suspicion. "If that's the case, then you're going to have to go through a decontamination process before you are even allowed back on the *Dixon*. You do understand that, right?"

"Affirmative," Murakame said. "We will be decontaminated. Just send us the ship."

"Roger that," del Mar said. "Sending the second dropship immediately. We'll all discuss what to do next once you are back on board, decontaminated, and able to better tell us what all happened down there."

The video feeds shut off. Dollarhyde continued to try reaching the *Dixon* again, but all they got was the same static that had kept them from communicating earlier.

"Okay, I'm totally confused," Bayne said. "Someone want to explain what just happened?"

Marsden was about to chime in and offer his best guess, but before he could Essentia spoke up. "I had an idea about what happened to Murakame, and I was about to tell Marsden about it before the video feeds kicked in. Now I don't think it's just an idea. I think I know exactly what happened."

"Well?" Llewellyn asked. "Are you going to tell us, or are you going to make us guess."

"Easy, Llewellyn," Marsden said. "Go ahead, Essentia. You found something in the Sten-Plus data files, didn't you?"

"I sure did. And if I'm right about this, and Murakame makes it back to the *Franklin Dixon*, then that will mean that the entire human race is screwed."

August 2, 2147 (Earth Calendar)
2016 Greenwich Mean Time
Location: Corridor of Sten-Plus Spacecraft, Outside of Power Core Room Three, Bullfinch-2
Marine Heartbeats Detected on Planet: 32

"Well that sounds omelet."

Llewellyn practically screamed at Bayne. "For the last time, you colossal idiot, it's *ominous*. It sounds *ominous*. And yeah, no shit it does. Jesus, just shut your damned moronic pie-hole for once!"

"Llewellyn!" Dollarhyde yelled. "You are out of line! Reign it in or else I'll order Conway to inject you with the same stuff she stuck into me, and you'll be facing disciplinary action when we get back. Do I make myself clear?"

Llewellyn took a deep breath. When she spoke again, it obviously took her a great deal of effort to sound calm. "Crystal clear, commander. It won't happen again."

"Good, marine. See that it doesn't." Dollarhyde looked to Essentia. "Tell us what you've got, and do it quickly. I suddenly get the very bad feeling that we're racing a clock here."

Essentia looked a bit perplexed by the outbursts that had interrupted her, but she regained her composure quickly. "It's the occupants of stasis field number thirty-seven," she said, once again reading from her PDM. "While the majority of the creatures that were held on the ship were taken exactly as they were found, the ship did have limited facilities for genetic engineering. The Sten-Plus took the occupants of stasis field thirty-six, which didn't appear to be any real threat to humans themselves, and then altered them."

"What was it about the aliens in thirty-six that didn't make them a threat?" Marsden said.

"It's not that they weren't a threat, it's just that they weren't a direct threat. They were parasites. Early tests showed that they were capable of infecting a number of animals that humans use as livestock. At first the Sten-Plus thought they could use this strain to damage our supply lines or possibly cause a famine. But I guess that wasn't fast enough for them. They re-engineered a number of the specimens to create the parasites that were in thirty-seven. Unlike thirty-six, this strain could infect humans."

"Tell us exactly what you mean when you say they can infect us," Dollarhyde said. "Would it be like some kind of disease that would kill us?"

"Worse," Essentia said. She paused to read more of the data, then hissed in a breath as she obviously didn't like what she saw. "Apparently they are pink and fleshy looking things that slightly resemble the human brain, except larger. Maybe the size of a very large, very loaded backpack. They attach to the back of their host, then proceed to, um, eat the host's nervous system."

"That doesn't sound very efficient of them," Marsden said.

"It sounds like a species that used to exist on Earth," Axel said. "*Cymothoa exigua*, also known as the tongue-eating louse. It lived in the ocean and would enter a fish's mouth, clamp itself down, and then proceed to eat and then replace the fish's tongue. They're believed to be extinct now, considering most of the fish species they preyed upon were overfished into nothing."

"Gross!" Bayne said. "You see, this is why I hate science. Nothing good ever comes from learning it."

Axel looked thoroughly horrified by that statement, and Marsden had the feeling that, even if Bayne really had had the slightest chance of getting together with her, he had just lost it.

"Is that what's going on?" Marsden asked Essentia. "Then replace the nervous system with themselves?"

"A large part of the nervous system at least. They completely devour and replace the host's spinal cord, and extend tendrils into the victim's brain. The parts of the brain that allow the host control of their own body are destroyed. But the worst part is that the parts of the brain that affect consciousness are left alone."

Marsden grimaced. "So you're saying that whoever gets infected with one of these things permanently loses the ability to live without it, yet at the same time they're completely aware that something has taken over their body and is controlling them?"

"That certainly seems to be what this data suggests," Essentia said.

"So wait," Llewellyn said. "Are you saying that one of us could be infected with some parasite controlling us against our will, and the rest of us wouldn't know?" From the way she eyed Bayne, Marsden could already guess the first person she would like to point a finger at as an imposter in their midst.

"No. Remember when I said about the parasite's size? It's not like it can hide that in someone's body. If the Thirty-Sevens act in the same way that the parasites in thirty-six did, then they will be clearly visible on the person's back."

"Not exactly an efficient method of hiding," Laughingmoon said.

"No," Marsden said. "Not unless you were, say, broadcasting using the small screen and camera of a PDM, in which case whoever was receiving the message wouldn't be able to see your back."

"So that's what we think happened to Murakame?" Hemingford asked. "Jesus. I always liked her. Very polite. That's one hell of a way to go."

"Are you sure there's no way at all to rescue someone once they've been taken over?" Marsden asked Essentia.

"There isn't, at least according to the limited tests the Sten-Plus could do. I mean, parts of the host's nervous system are just gone now. They permanently become puppets of these things."

"Is it just Murakame?" Bayne asked. "Or is it everyone else that got left behind in Delta team, too?"

"When Murakame sent her broadcast, she said that she and two others were still uninfected," Dollarhyde said. "I would actually bet money that there's three of them that have been taken over."

"Which means there's still seven members of Delta team that are unaccounted for," Conway said. "We might not be able to save the three taken over by the Thirty-Sevens, but we've still got to mount a rescue mission for the others."

"Don't worry, we're not dropping that as one of our objectives," Dollarhyde said. "But all this does mean we have to add one more, and we don't have a lot of time to do it in."

"I'm not following," Llewellyn asked. "Is it something to do with the dropship they requested?"

"Yeah, something about that doesn't sit right with me," Marsden said. "I think I could see what they're trying to do by getting back to the *Dixon*. Whatever it is these parasites do to spawn, they can make more of themselves and take over the crew of the Dixon, then head on back to the core planets. Except there's already a dropship here on the planet, and unless something terrible happened that none of us are aware of yet, it should still be in perfect flying condition."

"Two possibilities," Axel said as she looked at her own PDM. "The first would be that they need a pilot. It seems so far that the parasites only know whatever it is their hosts know, so if none of them have the skills to handle a drop ship, they would need someone to come down and get them, then infect that person before continuing. The problem with that scenario is that, of the two other marines who seem to be showing the exact same irregular vital signs as Murakame, both of them have basic flight training."

"So what's the other possibility?" Trieloff asked.

"The second possibility is that they need the extra room," Axel said. "One dropship wouldn't be enough for what they need."

"Why would they need that much room?" Hemingford asked. "One drop ship would be more than enough for just three of them."

"Unless they're not planning on it being just the three of them," Marsden said. "Either they have more parasites with them that need hosts, or they're planning on taking some of the creatures from this ship with them."

"Either way, things look really bad for humanity if they get back to the *Dixon*," Dollarhyde said. "How long is it going to take for the second dropship to land?"

"Given that the crew on the *Dixon* thinks this is an emergency, it will probably be on the ground in right around ten minutes," Marsden said. "But we probably have much more time than that. Whatever they want to load onto the two ships will take time."

Dollarhyde stood up. "Okay then, no more screwing around, everybody. We have three objectives and maybe a half an hour to complete all of them. Normally in this circumstance I'd suggest splitting up, but since we've still got an unknown number of monsters roaming around the ship wanting to turn us into Value Meals, we're going to have to stick together."

"We can't do all that as one group in time," Llewellyn said.

Dollarhyde's voice dropped and gave the order they had probably all been expecting, even though none of them would have wanted to admit it before now. "Priority one is stopping those parasites from reaching the *Dixon*. Priority two destroying this ship and any harmful biological matter still left on it. That means, against everything we believe in, our missing brothers and sisters have to be priority three. If we find them, we save them."

She didn't need to tell them what would happen if they didn't find the missing marines. They would go up with the ship. Marsden looked at his PDM and the life signs of the vanished marines. None of them looked like they were in good shape. For the first time, Marsden hoped, for their sakes, that they would die sooner rather than later. Blowing up with the ship would probably be painless, but they would still suffer up until that moment.

"Everyone off your asses and move out," Dollarhyde said. Her heart didn't seem to be in the order.

August 2, 2147 (Earth Calendar)
2021 Greenwich Mean Time
Location: Corridor of Sten-Plus Spacecraft,
Bullfinch-2
Marine Heartbeats Detected on Planet: 32

"From our current location, it looks like the quickest way out of the ship would be to head for the hole in the hull that we came in through," Essentia said. "Otherwise, we're starting to get enough of a map in our data that we could probably be able to get to the main door from here. That would allow us to get to Dropship Alpha faster."

Marsden listened to all this with only part of his attention. Although Dollarhyde was back in command at the moment, he'd taken the lead on their path down the corridor purely because he had one more eye to see danger than Dollarhyde did at this point.

"Any idea how close we might be getting to the second power core room?" Axel asked Essentia.

"Not a clue. We're approaching roughly the middle of the ship. If the three core rooms are evenly spaced out, then maybe we're almost there?"

Marsden looked up at the lights in the ceiling as several of them flickered. He hadn't seen any of the light sources do any such thing since the moment they'd turned the power back on, so he had to take that as a bad sign. The last time they'd been in a room that didn't have the correct amount of light, two of their people had become fertilizer.

"Something about the corridor ahead looks different," one of the marines said.

"It all looks weird-ass to me," Bayne said.

"No, look." Axel pointed at something on the wall up ahead. "The coloring is different." The group approached this oddity with a mix of speed and caution. Once they were closer, Marsden called for them to stop while he took a closer look. Something light and shimmery had been spread on the wall. It looked similar to the slime that had dripped from the plants on the ceiling, but it was a different consistency. In fact, there seemed to be a couple different consistencies of the stuff. All of it came in the shape of rope-like strands. In some spots the strands were thick while in others they were thin and fine. Looking ahead, Marsden found the substance in patches all along the corridor ahead with increasing frequency the farther he looked.

"What is it?" Dollarhyde asked him.

"I don't know," Marsden said. He pulled out one of his knives and touched the tip into one of the thicker patches of the substance. The knife went into the goop easily, but he had trouble pulling it back out. He had to actually put down his other weapons and grip the knife with both hands just to yank it free, and he hadn't even sunk the knife in that deep.

"Some kind of glue," Marsden said.

Curious about the thinner strands, he took the same knife and touched it to one of the thin gossamer strands. All Recon Marine knives were made with a special poly-carbonate steel that was supposed to withstand anything up to temperatures of nearly seven hundred degrees, yet the oh-so-thin strand sliced off the tip like a band saw through a weak piece of wood.

"Yikes," Laughingmoon said.

"There's a lot more patches of this stuff up ahead," Marsden said. "Maybe it would be better if we found a way around."

"I'm not sure that we have time for that," Dollarhyde said. "It doesn't look like any of the patches are so close together as to be impassable. We'll just have to step carefully. No one touch them, and try to keep quiet for the moment. Something did this, and we probably don't want to run into it."

They all proceeded to carefully make their way through the corridor, stepping gently when getting too close to the various filaments and patches. As they became more numerous, however, Marsden shot Dollarhyde several worried looks. While the stares Dollarhyde gave him back were even and calm, he could still tell that even she was wondering if this had been a good idea.

"I thinking we're getting close to the second power core room," Essentia said quietly. "Unless the rooms are laid out in an asymmetrical pattern throughout the ship, my best guess is that the next one will be two side corridors ahead and to the right.

"What do you think?" Dollarhyde asked Axel. "Will destroying two power cores be enough?"

"I don't even know that my charges would be enough to destroy one power core," Axel said. "But given our new priorities, I think we need to risk it. If my explosives fail to destroy the ship, then we'll just have to come back after stopping the Thirty-Sevens."

"And if that happens, we still might be able to rescue the remaining marines," Conway said. Suddenly she paused and gestured for everyone else to stop and be quiet. With their footsteps no longer echoing through the lonely corridors, all that any of them could hear was a slight, high-pitched whine from the energy coursing through the walls to power the overhead lights. After several seconds of standing there, Dollarhyde carefully stepped around a particularly large patch of the willowy goop so that she could stand right next to Conway.

"What is it?" Dollarhyde asked.

"Maybe... maybe it's nothing," Conway said with a distinct

note of disappointment. "I could have sworn I heard—"

"…help…"

The single word was faint and breathless, the kind of thing that could have easily been attributed to the imagination if it wasn't clearly evident that every single one of the marines heard it. Conway looked for a moment like she was going to dash on ahead, her medic instincts automatically kicking into gear at the sound of someone in distress, but Dollarhyde put a hand to her chest and held her back.

"No," Dollarhyde said quietly. "We all go together, and stay careful. Everything about this stinks of being a trap."

Conway looked unhappy but nodded. They resumed their movements, gently picking their way through the minefield of slimy booby traps on the walls, floor, and ceiling around them. At one point Axel put a hand on Marsden's shoulder and pulled him back a few centimeters. He had no idea why she would do this until he saw a single strand of the silky filament hanging down in from of him from the ceiling. It was so thin that he hadn't even been able to see it until it was pointed out to him, and if that one strand acted in the same way as the stuff he'd seen earlier, if he had walked into it the strand would have lacerated his face. Marsden nodded his thanks to Axel for seeing it first, then carefully went around it and resolved to pay even closer attention to his environment than he already had been.

"…help… please…" At those words everyone again stopped. Marsden looked back at Conway to see her visibly shaking with the strain not to run ahead, but his own close call had shown everyone else just how much folly that would be.

"That sounds like it could be Arizona," Trieloff whispered. Conway promptly took out her PDM and looked up Arizona's vital signs.

"Whatever's wrong with her, it's different than Murakame," Conway said. "Too-rapid heartbeat. Low oxygen levels. Brainwave patterns suggest an incredible amount of pain. Christ. Whatever's happening to her, her pain must be off the scale. I've never seen anything like this."

"And the other missing members of Delta team?" Dollarhyde asked.

"The other six that aren't like Murakame, let's see," Conway said. "Yes. The same basic patterns. Something very horrible is happening to them. Did anyone get any idea where her voice came from?"

"It sounded to me like it was down the same hall we need to go to reach the second power core," Essentia said.

"Okay, Essentia, figure out what we're about to deal with. Everyone else, make one hundred percent sure you're ready for a battle," Dollarhyde said. She paused. "Is it just a coincidence that this is happening in a power core room again?"

"Probably not," Axel said. "We already believed that the spores for the killer plants were attracted to energy. We have no idea what the Sten-Plus use to power their ships, but at this point it seems like a likely hypothesis that their power source is something that life forms find attractive."

"I don't think it's attractive," Bayne mumbled. "I think this is all pretty ugly."

"I think maybe I've got a hit here," Essentia said, "but I don't think the information is going to be very useful to us. Most of this is in a portion of the data files that either hasn't been translated yet, or something in the alien syntax is giving the translation program a problem. There's references to two creatures that can emit either a sticky or fibrous substance." She gestured as the strange goo all around them. "It's a mating pair, male and female, or whatever equivalent to male and female their species happen to have."

"Anything else?" Dollarhyde asked. "Anything at all?"

"No. Everything else in the file is still incomprehensible."

"Alright then, everyone, you heard her," Dollarhyde said. "Two targets with some kind of defensive attack, and seven marines in distress. Axel, be ready to place your charges, as we might need to get out of there quickly."

They went down the last corridor to the core room with Marsden still taking point. Just outside the door they stopped, and Marsden did his best to see inside the room without actually sticking his head through the entryway. He pulled back and whispered what he'd seen to the others.

"Looks almost identical to the previous power core room, including another exit on the other side. The lights are dim, but not as much as in the previous room. That seems to be from more of that goop on the ceiling. In fact the entire room is covered in it except for a few thin paths on the floor here and there. No sign of either of our targets or any of the hostages."

"No sign at all?" Conway asked. "We all heard Arizona. She's got to be in there."

Dollarhyde gingerly stepped ahead of Marsden. Gesturing for everyone else to be ready to shoot if anything happened, she then called through the door. "Arizona? Anyone? Are you in there?"

They all braced for some kind of attack at Dollarhyde's intrusion on the quiet, but for several seconds there was nothing. Finally someone, not Arizona, said, "Dollarhyde. Help."

Dollarhyde nodded her okay to the marines, and they all filed in using a tight defensive pattern that kept them from spreading out and getting stuck in the slime and filaments. Still there was no movement in the room, and no sign of any of the marines.

What he did see, however, were a number of ghastly, bloated flesh sacks plastered on the walls all over the room. Marsden's first thought was that they were some kind of larva or egg sacs, in which case he wanted to spare no time shooting each and every one before they could become something worse. But as his eyes adjusted to the dimmer light, Marsden realized he didn't need to wait for them to be something out of his most horrifying nightmares. Each flesh sac wiggled and squirmed, obviously alive, but it was the number that horrified him.

Looking around the room, he saw exactly seven of them. They'd found the missing members of Delta team.

"...help..." This plea was Arizona again, and Marsden realized that she was the closest of the seven flesh sacs that hung on the wall about four meters from them. And it wasn't that she was inside the flesh sac. She *was* the flesh sac. Her body was swollen to nearly three times its original girth. Arizona's clothes and armor had either been stripped from her or else had ripped apart and fallen at her feet in the process that caused her body to hideously balloon. Her skin was tight and stretched against whatever was inside her, so much that in places Marsden thought the greasy, sweat-soaked skin had gone translucent and allowed him to see some kind of thick fluid sloshing inside her just below the surface. Her face was completely unrecognizable, and if not for her faint calls for rescue, Marsden wouldn't have had any idea which of the marines she was. Another quick glance around told him that all the marines were in the exact same condition.

Marsden wanted to puke, and he was sure that he wasn't alone. Llewellyn made a few sounds that clearly said she was fighting back a gagging reflex, but she managed to keep control of herself. There would be plenty of time later to vomit up their rations when they figured out what to do here, if there even was such a possibility.

"Oh God," Conway whispered. "This is monstrous." She took a first tentative step toward Arizona. Dollarhyde put a hand on her shoulder to stop her, which Conway immediately shoved away. "Don't you dare try to stop me, Dollarhyde."

"Conway, I don't think there's anything you can do for them anymore," Dollarhyde said. She hefted her MH-56. "The best we can do for them is put them out of their misery as quickly as possible."

"Uh-uh. No," Conway said. "The very least you can let me do is examine her first. There's got to be something I can do as long as they're still alive. Maybe if I made incisions in key places, I can drain whatever fluid is causing this."

Marsden was pretty sure that simply draining the fluid wouldn't be enough to save them, considering how hideously distorted their body features had become. As he was staring at Arizona, he finally noticed something he hadn't before. Hanging right over Arizona, in a shape that looked partly like a net and partly like a web, there was a concentrated patch of the razor-thin filaments. They looked almost like they had been put there on purpose to create an awning over her.

Marsden looked around to the other marines, noticing that Axel did the same thing. Both of them saw at the same time that there was a similar net over every one of the incapacitated marines. Not only that, but now that he was looking for them, Marsden saw thing strands actually hanging in the air and connecting each of the net awnings. The filaments were pulled tight, like tripwires.

Tripwires? Marsden turned his head to Axel and saw that she must have been thinking the exact same thing.

Conway moved to get closer to Arizona.

"Conway, no!" Marsden screamed. Before he could even finish getting the words out, Conway hissed and looked down at her foot. Her boot had been sliced open by something, and blood was freely pouring out. Marsden saw the razor filament she had walked into, which was connected to a point on the wall, which then went up, right to...

The net dropped from its place on the wall. It was so light, so thin, that it did fall with any speed. If he were the kind to think of things in such ways, he might have described it as having a gentle whimsy as it fell, like a loose spider web drifting in a slight spring breeze. He didn't have time to look at the others, but he was pretty sure all of the other filament nets had also been triggered to fall.

What Marsden did have time for was to grab the two marines nearest him, Dollarhyde and Essentia, and violently shove them back, simultaneously pushing everyone behind them back in the direction of the door they'd come in. He looked back just in time to see the net gently waft into place on the swollen flesh of Arizona's head.

The filament sliced through her stretched-tight skin, and with the pressure that had built up from inside her body, Arizona exploded.

Her body seemed to evaporate in much the same way an over-full water balloon would burst, the tears in her head expanding outward like across her skin with lightning-quick speed. Noxious green fluid spewed from her along with pieces of organs and bone. Marsden felt some droplets of the liquid hit his back and sizzle as it tried to dissolve through his clothing. It didn't get far, but as he looked back he saw that Conway hadn't been so lucky. All seven of the marines burst throughout the room, but Conway was the only person close enough to the exploding bodies to get a full, direct hit. For a brief second she managed to scream when the substance hit her face, but the green acid instantly ate through her skin, her nose, her eyes, her tongue. Conway fell back to the floor with half her head and a significant portion of her chest gone.

"Back!" Dollarhyde screamed. "Everyone back through the door!" They were trained for this kind of hasty retreat, but several of the marines must have forgotten about the sticky spots and razor filaments. Trieloff made the mistake of backing up into a spot that glued her boots in place while two other marines ran afoul of dangling filament threads. One was caught right in the throat, causing the person next to him to get doused in a shower of his arterial blood, while the other suddenly developed a deep penetrating gash in his side. It caused him to lose his balance, making him fall into a thicker patch of the strands. The sliced through him like he'd been put into one of those old-fashioned hard-boiled egg slicers, turning him into tiny chunks of unrecognizable flesh.

Before any of them could make it as far as the door, something shot out from some unknown place overhead. A huge glob of the sticky version of the substance smacked into the top of the door from, dripping down and creating long strands of glue that barred their way. Marsden turned to the other door just in time to see a wad of the filament do the same thing, some of it slicing into the material of the ship while the rest dangled over the door.

"Look up there!" Axel called. She pointed in the direction of the top of the power core, where two creatures had apparently been hiding the entire time. Each of them looked like some kind of insect with heavily armored exoskeletons. The number and spacing of their legs made Marsden think of spiders, while their heads and bodies were more reminiscent of wasps, complete with gnashing mandibles in front and enormous stingers in their rears.

One was brighter in color but significantly smaller, measuring about the same as Bayne's shoulder width from mouth to stinger. The other was a drab gray and huge, easily the length of two marines lying down end to end.

"Everyone, you know what to do!" Dollarhyde screamed. "Fire!"

Almost everyone turned their rifles to the wasp-spiders perched in the center of the room. The only two who didn't were Axel, who was ducking and weaving among the filaments in an effort to get closer to the core as she pulled out a couple of charges, and Trieloff, who was still struggling to get out from where she'd gotten stuck. She only struggled for a moment before bending low to untie her boots.

Marsden was afraid for a moment what might happen as seventeen separate marines tried to shoot something on top of a power core coursing with unknown energies and technology, but the two wasp-spiders jumped away from their spot quickly, each of them landing on and sticking to the walls on either side of the room. Neither of them seemed deterred by the glue or razor strands, and they walked among it all easily without sticking or getting cut open. Before most of the marines could adjust their aim, each of the creatures opened up their mandibles and spit something from their mouths. The gob from the larger one (the female, Marsden guessed, based on what little he knew of Earth insects) was big enough to hit three marines at once. The sticky substance covered their faces and knocked them off their feet, causing them to splat against the floor and stay there, unable to move or breathe for the glue.

The smaller one, likely the male, spit a wad of the strange silky strands that hit another marine square in her chest. She didn't even get the chance to scream before the filament ripped apart her breasts, ribcage, and lungs.

"They're too fast!" one of the marines yelled as the female again leaped to a different section of the wall. He was rewarded for his observation with a blast of the female's glue against his chest, which knocked him back into a batch of filament. The filament ripped apart his back and rifle, but it didn't appear to kill him outright. Instead he found himself glued to a wall. All the other marines tried to adjust their positions to get a better angle on the female as she jumped off the wall and directly in front of the marine she had just incapacitated.

Most of them aimed and fired at the female at the same time. She didn't make any move to get out of their way this time, instead keeping all of her concentration on her trapped prey. The first several shots they took hit her in the abdomen, and while they punched a couple of holes in her body large enough to profusely bleed with black ichor, she didn't pay much attention to them. The male, on the other hand, made some kind of wheezy hiss in warning at them before jumping between them and his mate.

While the male acted as a living shield, the female reared up on four of its hind legs to expose its stinger. The trapped marine screamed out a final challenge about what he wanted to do to the wasp-spider's mother before the female stabbed him in the stomach. The marine grunted in pain, trying not to make any more noise as he faced his death, but he couldn't help but scream as the wasp-spider injected him with something. His body instantly began to swell into an earlier version of what they had seen with Arizona and the others. The female seemed to lose a lot of its strength as she pumped him full of the poison and acid, and once he was swelled to bursting the female jumped away, although with decidedly less vigor than before. The male, significantly injured by their rain of bullets at this point, also leaped away, turning in midair just in time to spit another wad of filament.

The marines were too close to the exploding sac of flesh this time. Four of them were in the path of the acid splash, and while one was just far enough away she only got bathed on one side, it was still enough to dissolve most of her leg and drop her to the floor. Although she was obviously dying, she continued to aim and fire up until the moment she expired.

"I've got three charges placed!" Axel yelled. "Let's get out of here!"

"In case you haven't noticed, we're still kind of trapped in this room!" Llewellyn said back.

"I'm on that too," Axel said. "Just don't let either of those things get me while I set this up."

"Whatever you're planning on doing, you better get it done five minutes ago!" Dollarhyde said. "If you take more than half a minute, I don't think there's going to be any of us left!"

To the marines' advantage, both of the wasp-spiders had slowed significantly. Marsden guessed that the female would have to take some time before she built up enough acid in her stinger again to pull the same trick, while the male was running with an obvious limp in several of its legs. They all kept their fire on the creatures, trying to herd them into a corner, while Axel knelt down a safe distance from the strands over the opposite door. She pulled a long, thin strip out of her supplies, unrolled it, and then tossed one end in the direction of deadly curtain blocking their escape. The filaments sliced off a small portion of the end, but Axel didn't seem to mind that. She pulled out a small device with a rather large button on it, which she wired up to the end of the strip that was closest to her.

"Fire in the hole!" she yelled as she made a fist and smashed it down on the button. She rolled out of the way as the whole strip ignited with a bright flash. At first Marsden didn't understand what that had done. Then he saw the way flames began to lick at the place where the strip and the filaments met. It made sense, he suddenly realized. They couldn't throw or shoot anything at the strands without the object being sliced into pieces, but the wispiness of the material made it susceptible to fire.

"Just hold those things off long enough for the fire to burn all the way, and then we can get out!" Axel said. She ran back to help Trieloff get out of her boots without further stepping in the glue while everyone else continued to unload their magazines into the wasp-spiders. The male finally went down, its legs curling up against it just like the death throes of a terrestrial spider, but while slow, the female was still going strong. She didn't look like she could do her leaping anymore, so instead she turned directly for them and charged.

"The door's open now!" Dollarhyde said. She didn't need to say anything else to get the rest of them headed for the exit. Axel led the way with Trieloff beside her, while Marsden and Bayne brought up the rear. They wasted no time getting out the door and to the end of the hallway, where there were still stick and dangerous spots, but it wasn't as thick here as it had been in the other hallway.

The wasp-spider didn't follow them.

Marsden took a deep breath, only realizing now how much his lungs burned from the exertion of the battle they'd just thought.

"I don't think it's going to follow us," Bayne muttered.

"Don't bet on it," Marsden said. "Just get ready, everyone. The instant you see it in the doorway, you unload everything you can into it.

They all stopped. They waited. Several seconds passed.

With renewed energy, the female spider-wasp appeared in the doorway and sprinted down the hallway at them.

They let loose an insane rain of bullets down the hall, but for several seconds the wasp-spider just kept going. It was halfway down the corridor before it even began to slow down. Still they all kept their fingers on their triggers. It kept lurching forward, desperate to get one final attack in on them. It never got that last chance.

It collapsed just two meters from them. As black sludge leaked out of the impossible number of holes in its body, the female wasp-spider curled up for one last time and was still.

August 2, 2147 (Earth Calendar)
2040 Greenwich Mean Time
Location: Corridor of Sten-Plus Spacecraft
Outside Power Core Room 2, Bullfinch-2
Marine Heartbeats Detected on Planet: 14

Forty-six. That was the number of Recon Marines that had landed on planet Bullfinch-2 to look into the crashed ship of an unknown species. It was the number that kept repeating over and over in Marsden's head as he looked around at the only people out of those forty-six that had survived up to this point: Marsden himself, Dollarhyde, Axel, Trieloff, Bayne, Chunda, Llewellyn, Laughingmoon, Hemingford, and Essentia. Ten marines were all that were left. Marsden had been on missions that had gone south before, and he had seen plenty of comrades in arms die in the line of duty, but he had never experienced anything like this. And the mission still wasn't over.

"We plain and simple don't have the time to try getting to the last power core room," Dollarhyde said as they all took a minute to catch their breaths and reload their weapons. They'd come down with plenty of reloads to spare, but now, after the amount of ammunition they'd been forced to go through just to get out of the last room alive, it seemed entirely possible that they could run out of bullets long before they ran out of enemies. "We're going to have to just see if what Axel's already put down will be enough to blow the ship and everything on it."

"I have the trigger all set up and ready," Axel said as she indicated a small case clipped next to her PDM. "All it needs is to be armed. If anything happens to me, one of you will have to take if from my dead body."

"That's not going to happen," Bayne grumbled.

"I certainly hope that's true, but you all need to know just in case."

"Duly noted," Dollarhyde said. "Conway, give us a status update on…" She paused as she realized what she had just said. She had to take another deep breath before speaking again. "Someone check their PDM and give us a status update on the three that were infected by the Thirty-Sevens. I'd check my own, but it looks like the screen might have gotten splashed by some of that acid."

"At least it's still recording your vitals," Chunda said as he pulled his own PDM out. "The PDMs are still registering Murakame and the others as being on the planet. There's an extra heartbeat on the planet now, Singh, but her vitals are looking as poor as the others."

"She must have been the pilot that got sent down with Dropship Beta, and now she's been taken over as well," Marsden said.

"Which means we only have as much time left as it takes for them to load up whatever they're taking onto the two dropships," Dollarhyde said. "Essentia, how close are we to one of the two exits?"

"Very close," Essentia said. "If we were to run we could make it in less than five minutes."

"But also if we run," Llewellyn said, "we could go headlong into some other kind of trap. If we hit one more room like the last one, we're all dead and the human race might very well be doomed."

"We don't want that," Bayne said. "Doomed is bad."

"We go as fast as we can and still keep our guard up," Dollarhyde said. "Marsden and Bayne, you two take point.

Llewellyn and Laughingmoon take the rear. Take nothing for granted. We have no guarantee that we're still going to run into anything, but we know that all those creatures are still out there."

They formed up and moved all of a meter forward before Dollarhyde said something else. "Wait! Everyone stop."

"Uh, why?" Bayne asked.

Then it hit them all. There was a skunk smell in the air. And it was growing stronger, stronger—

"Cover!" Dollarhyde yelled.

If Hairy had come at them from ahead like it had last time, they probably all would have survived the initial attack. Instead the ones in the rear weren't quite fast enough by a matter of half a second. As the majority of the marines threw themselves against the wall to get out of Hairy's way, Llewellyn, Laughingmoon, and Trieloff were hit by the thing blurring past them. Llewellyn and Laughingmoon were gone in a bloody flash, pieces of them flying everywhere and showering the others. Trieloff had managed a half turn away before Hairy blew through the corridor. Instead of hitting her head on, Hairy buzzed against her back. The entire back of her uniform and all the skin along her spine were flayed off her, and the force of the hit sent her flying headfirst into the wall, where all of them distinctly heard a sickening crack as her neck snapped.

"God damn it!" Dollarhyde screamed after the thing as it vanished somewhere down the hall ahead. "I am getting seriously sick of you, you bastard. Next time I smell you, you're going down!"

Marsden thought he heard something far ahead, so far they couldn't quite see, but he almost thought it sounded like something skidding to the a halt. The stink, which had started to fade, suddenly came back to all their nostrils.

"I think it heard you, Dollarhyde," Marsden said.

"Aim down the hall and just start shooting!" Dollarhyde said. "Do it now before it…"

They all started firing as the stench increased. At the last second, like a matador dodging a pull, Marsden dove to the side and hoped that everyone behind him had managed to do the same. From the shower of blood he felt at his back, though, he knew that wasn't the case. He turned to see Chunda's severed head smack against the wall and bounce to the floor, his eyes still wide with what looked like consciousness for nearly a second before they went dull with death. The rest of his body was gone. Dollarhyde had also been hit, but it looked like a glancing blow to her side. Marsden thought she would be okay up until the moment where she clutched her side and the blood started to flow from the wound in thick rivulets. She leaned against the wall and slid to the ground.

"Shit. It looks like that's me done," Dollarhyde said, her voice an uncharacteristic whisper.

Marsden stooped down next to her and tried to throw one of her arms over his should so he could support her. They'd left the makeshift stretcher some distance behind them, not that they would have had the time to secure her to it again anyway. Although the smell had faded, it wasn't completely gone. Hairy was somewhere down the hallway still, and it was looking like the creature might come back at any moment.

"Come on, we can still get you out of here," Marsden said. Dollarhyde, however, slapped away any of the marines' attempts at a helping hand.

"I'd only slow you down, and none of you have any time for that," Dollarhyde said.

"Dollarhyde, we're not going to just leave you behind,"

Hemingford said. "That's not the way we work."

"Yeah, and that particular code of ethics worked really well for us when we went looking for Arizona and the others, didn't it?" Dollarhyde said. "Besides, no one's going to want to see my ugly half-a-mug back on the core worlds anyway. I'll scare little children."

"You already scare little children," Marsden said. To his surprise, Dollarhyde smiled at that, or at least as much of a smile as she could still manage with only half her mouth.

"Damned straight I do. Now enough with the witty banter. Bayne, give me your chain gun."

"But... but... that's mine," Bayne said. Marsden didn't think his face would ever be capable of such an expression, but Bayne actually pouted.

"We can get you another one if we live," Marsden said. "Do as she says."

Bayne shrugged off his pack that fed the chain gun, then placed the enormous weapon with surprising tenderness in Dollarhyde's hands. "Take good care of it," Bayne said, then thought about it and added, "for all the ten seconds where you're still going to exist."

The angle of the gun was awkward from her position on the floor, but she managed to hold it upright despite her waning strength and aim it down the corridor. "Now get the hell out of here, you idiots," Dollarhyde said. "You've got an entire human race to save from brain-eating parasites."

"They don't actually eat brains," Axel said. "As Essentia explained, what they do is—"

"Axel, now is really not the time for you to get technical," Marsden said. "Alright, everyone, you heard her! Move!"

As much as Marsden knew they should still be careful, he

was pretty sure they no longer had that luxury. He ran down the hall, away from Dollarhyde, and didn't look back at either the marines that followed him or his current commanding officer as she sat in the middle of the hall and waiting for her last stand.

"Okay, Hairy! Come and get me!" Dollarhyde yelled back down the corridor. "Let's see if you're faster than this!"

Even as they ran, they all smelled the pungent stink as Hairy started back toward them. At almost the same time, the heavy metallic roar of the chain gun started. Just underneath it, Marsden could hear Dollarhyde's manic battle cries in her last moments.

The chain gun stopped just as the stink let up. Their PDMs all buzzed with the news that another marine heartbeat had vanished.

No one looked back. They just kept running.

August 2, 2147 (Earth Calendar)
2044 Greenwich Mean Time
Location: Corridor to the Main Entryway, Sten-
Plus Spacecraft, Bullfinch-2
Marine Heartbeats Detected on Planet: 9

They knew they were approaching the main entryway for two reasons. One, the corridor had grown wider and was obviously intended to have more traffic. Two, they now started to find the dead bodies of a variety of fantastic, monstrous creatures

"What happened here?" Heming ford asked as they stepped past the carcass of something that resembled an eight-meter-long boa constrictor with twenty legs.

Axel paused only long enough to examine the marks on the carcass. "I'd say those are battle wounds."

"Battle wounds against what?" Bayne asked.

"All of the creatures that were released were specifically gathered by the Sten-Plus because they would be particularly harmful to humans," Marsden said. "But that doesn't exactly mean that they were going to play nice with each other. If all of these creatures were released at once, it stands to reason that some of them didn't wait to find us before their combat or self-preservation habits kicked in."

Not too much farther down the path, they found another one of the many-legged snake creatures, this time surrounded the corpses of a small pack of creatures that would have appeared similar to mice if fully half their bodies didn't consist of teeth. Given the bulges in the snake-thing, Marsden had to guess that it managed to eat some of the little creatures before they got their revenge on it. The joke appeared to be on them in the end, though, as every one of the teeth-mice looked like it had died soon after taking a bite out of the larger predator.

"It must have been poisonous," Axel said as she looked at the dead creatures.

"Yeah, see that greasy coat all over the snake-thing?" Essentia asked. "Hold on." She stopped to root around in her supplies.

"I don't know what you think you're doing, but we don't have time," Hemingford said.

"There's always time for science," Essentia muttered as she found a small stoppered vial that had been used to carry emergency water rations earlier. Axel grunted her approval with the sentiment as Essentia pulled out the stopper. "Pretty much all the biological samples we could have gotten from the trip are going to be destroyed. I'm sure the Science Corp would be very appreciative if we at least manage to bring back something." She collected a small amount of the greasy substance in the vial, being careful not to get any on her skin just in case it proved fatal just through contact, and then stopped it back up and put it in a safe place in her supplies.

The closer they got to the entrance, the greater the carnage they found. Many of the creatures they found were relatively smaller, being roughly human-sized, but they did find a number of dead alien bodies of significantly greater size. Marsden pushed them past most of it, reminding them all that they didn't know how much time they might still have, but even he had to stop and pause at the enormous hoofed and feathered creature lying directly in front of the main entrance. The thing's head was a massive tangle of horns and it had an extremely long, whip-like tale covered in what looked like needles. It was roughly half the size of a dropship, and if the thing had been healthy and hearty, it probably would have completely killed all the remaining Recon Marines currently under his command. As it was, it still breathed, its huge flanks pulsing irregularly as it tried to suck in air, and there were an uncountable number of bullet-holes in its side, right along with the kind of scorch-marks that could have only been caused by incendiary grenades. Axel, of course, took the most note of this latter detail.

"These were very inexpertly aimed," Axel said as the beast took its last shuddering breath. Whatever had happened to it, it must have been recent if it hadn't even had the chance to die yet. "Murakame would have had a number of incendiary grenades on her, but she would have known better how to target something like this with them."

"Maybe this thing was too fast for her to get her attacks off correctly," Essentia said.

"That could be," Marsden said. "Or maybe these parasites aren't as good at using their host's skills as we thought they were."

"That might make sense," Axel said. "She obviously wasn't very good at faking being normal during her first broadcast to us."

"She seemed to be better at it the second time," Hemingford said. "So maybe the more they use their host, the easier for it is for them to use their host's abilities."

"If we're lucky, that will apply to their ability to fly a dropship, too," Marsden said. "But hopefully we won't need to rely on that."

The main entryway was still open, and local night had started to fall on the area, bathing the inside of the open door with an eerie pink and purple light. This light made it hard enough for them to see that they almost missed that there was the dead body of a Recon Marine lying just beyond the hulking, horned beast. It was one of the marines who'd disappeared along with Murakame, and he would have been flat on his back if his back had still been flat. Instead his body lolled to the side to made room for the enormous pink protrusion coming from his back.

Essentia's description of the Thirty-Sevens earlier had been enough to give Marsden a vivid mental image of what they looked like, but that didn't even compare to the instinctual revulsion that the parasite brought to Marsden once he actually saw it. Just as they'd surmised, the parasite was low enough on the marine's back anyone looking at him head on wouldn't have seen it. From the side, however, the brain-like monstrosity bulged out like an impossible, twisted tumor. Various tentacle-like appendages went from the parasite to the places where it anchored into the marine's body. The parasite had more or less shredded the back of the marine's uniform and armor to get at the soft flesh underneath, and where the tentacles met the skin there were large, unsightly lesions and bruises.

The parasite also had a huge gash down the center that looked like it had come from a strike by the horned-beast's tale.

"So they can be killed," Marsden said. "That's very good to know."

"If he's dead, then why am I still reading his life signs on my PDM?" Essentia asked. Marsden checked his own PDM and saw that she was right. The parasite was clearly dead, but the marine still have a very faint heartbeat and some brainwave activity.

"Are you sure that everything you said earlier about the host not being able to live without the parasite is correct?" Marsden asked Essentia.

"No, I'm not, but the Sten-Plus certainly seemed to think that would be the case."

"Maybe we can still save him if we get that thing off his

back," Bayne said. Marsden figured it was worth a try, so he took out one of his knives and gingerly tried to slide it between the flesh of the parasite and the ravaged skin of the marine's back.

"No, stop," Essentia said as she stared at her PDM. "Now try it again." Marsden did as she said, and once again ceased when she told him to. "Every time you try to separate it from him, his heartbeat gets worse. There's probably something in the parasite's physiology that automatically tries to kill the host if it's removed."

"So what do we do instead?" Hemingford asked.

Marsden stooped down next to the marine's head and forced one of his eyes open. While everything else about the marine made him look like an empty shell, Marsden could have sworn that he still saw some fire in the man's eyes.

"I think he's still conscious," Marsden said. "He knows that we're here." He looked over to Axel and made a slight motion with his head, hoping that she would understand what he was trying to tell her without words. She wasn't usually the kind who was that kind at interpreting non-verbal signals, but she was the one he most wanted doing this. Thankfully she seemed to get it, and she nodded almost imperceptibly before going around the fallen marine and stooping behind him, where the marine wouldn't be able to see. Judging from the knowing flash Marsden thought he saw in the marine's eye, though, this man knew exactly what was about to happen and preferred it to the voiceless, unending torment he was currently going through.

Axel pulled out a sidearm, checked to make sure it was loaded, and then aimed it at the back of the marine's head.

Marsden looked at the marine's nametag. Lapinsky. Marsden barely knew the man, but when he looked over at Essentia he realized that she did. And judging from the shininess in at the edge of her eyes, he guessed that she knew him well.

"Goodbye, Lapinsky," Essentia said quietly. Essentia, rather than Marsden, was the one to look at Axel and nodded her head.

Axel ended the man's suffering.

August 2, 2147 (Earth Calendar)
2049 Greenwich Mean Time
Location: Main Entryway of the Sten-Plus
Spacecraft, Bullfinch-2
Marine Heartbeats Detected on Planet: 8

Other than Lapinsky, there were no signs of the Thirty-Sevens near the main entryway, nor were there any signs that traps or ambushes had been left for them when they tried to get out of the ship. Nonetheless, Marsden made sure that the last four Recon Marines under his command moved with the utmost caution as they walked out the main entryway. As soon as their boots touched the rocky, unforgiving surface of the planet, Marsden had to fight an overwhelming urge to drop to his knees and kiss the surface of Bullfinch-2 as a thank you for no longer being the Sten-Plus ship. At any other time, he might have done it anyway just to be an over-acting smartass, but for the moment he was in command and he had to set a precedent for the others.

That was why he chided Bayne for doing the exact same thing Marsden had just been thinking about doing, but was secretly pleased that at least someone had done it.

Under three hours had passed since they'd entered the spacecraft, but everything around them seemed changed, like they had someone gone from the harmless, barren world where'd they'd started to some kind of nightmare hellscape. With this impression firmly in mind, they didn't go down the most direct path to where they had left Dropship Alpha. Instead Marsden directed them to a line of uneven rocks nearby that looked like they would hide their approach for most of the way back.

Everyone stayed quiet, all attempts at witty banter to lighten the mood completely gone. Marsden couldn't speak for anyone else, but the full weight of how unbelievably awful this mission had been was only now settling on him. The Recon Marines' small army of private psychologists and therapists would have a field day with those of them, if any, that managed to get off this rock.

Their path kept them pretty well hidden up until the moment where they could see the two dropships. If they went any farther they would lose their cover, but their spot at least afforded them a decent view of what was going on. Dropship Beta had landed a safe distance away from the first dropship, making it harder for them to see, but most of the interesting action seemed to be happening at Dropship Alpha. They could see all three of the remaining infected marines. Singh, the pilot that had come down with Beta was just coming down the gangway from inside. Nooner, the other infected marine, was lifting up some kind of bright blue bubble from the ground. It was one of about twenty of the bubbles, and they all looked strikingly similar to the stasis cages in which the creatures of the Sten-Plus's ark had originally been kept. Unlike those stasis bubbles from earlier, however, these were all the same size. Marsden wasn't the only one to notice this.

"Those bubbles look like they'd be just the right size to each hold one of the parasites, don't you think?" Essentia asked.

"Affirmative," Axel said. "We're at approximately a two to one chance that we were right about their plan. They have more of the parasites ready."

"Definitely more than enough to infect the remaining people on the *Franklin Dixon*," Marsden said. "And that's just the number we can see. We have no idea how many they've already loaded inside. They've probably been spending most of this time hauling all of them out here to the dropships."

"If those are the last of them, we don't have much time left," Hemingford said.

"No, not much, but still enough to formulate a plan," Marsden said. "Come on, everyone, quick thinking. What have we got at our disposal and how can we use it?"

"We've all got our MH-56s still," Essentia said, "although ammo is limited. Several side arms and knives…"

"And a whole crapton of explosives," Axel said.

"Okay, seriously, I've got to ask, Axel," Bayne said. "Where do you even keep all these grenades and charges and thermite strips and whatever?"

"Anywhere they'll fit."

Marsden immediately saw how this could go into less than appropriate territory for the situation, and he waved Bayne off from commenting further. "And you've still got the detonator for the explosives on the ship?" Marsden asked.

Axel pulled it out and set it on the ground between where they were all crouched. "Right here. I'm ready for the fireworks show whenever you are."

"We still don't know how well those are going to work," Hemingford said. "They might not even make a dent in the power cores."

"Or they could turn us all into nuclear particles," Essentia said.

"If the former happens, then too bad," Marsden said. "We'll just have to make sure we survive this and come back with a way to wipe it all out for real. If the latter happens, well, I sure don't want to die any more than any of you, but you have to admit that nuking the entire site would definitely take care of that pesky potential danger to the entire human race."

"So you want me to trigger it?" Axel asked as she reached for the detonator again. Marsden stopped her hand before it got there.

"No, not yet. Look back at the dropships. See how they're all working at carrying the bubbles into Dropship Alpha?"

Essentia looked back in that direction. "All except Murakame. She's off to the side. It looks like she's pulling out her PDM and is getting ready to send another message to the *Dixon*."

"My point is that all of them have put down their weapons to do what they're doing. For this exact moment, we're armed and they're not. They're also distracted. We have the element of surprise at the moment, and maybe we can even increase that surprise."

He told them all his plan. As plans went, it wasn't complex. No one would ever say Marsden should be promoted to the highest ranks of command with simplistic attacks like this. But sometimes simple was the best.

Right as he was finishing, the PDMs buzzed with the news that Murakame was again trying to contact the *Dixon*. Marsden hesitated for only a moment before using his own PDM to listen in, but he turned down the volume as low as he could while still hearing it. When others moved to do the same, Marsden waved them off. They were far enough away and just hidden enough that Murakame and the others shouldn't have been able to hear the echo of their message on other nearby PDMs, but Marsden didn't want to risk it at the moment. In fact, this would be exactly the moment he was hoping for to catch the Thirty-Sevens off guard.

"Come in, *Franklin Dixon*, this is Murakame," Murakame said. Yet again, her inflection was less stilted than the time before. Each time she made the effort to communicate with someone else, she sounded more human. To Marsden's relief, though, the Dixon was already clued in that something was up.

"Murakame, this is del Mar. What the hell is going on down there? Singh wasn't down for more than a few minutes before we detected a radical change in her vital signs."

"We're under attack from the parasite-infected marines," Murakame said. "Singh was injured. We're on our way back up. It's imperative that you attack the site from orbit once we're almost at the *Dixon*."

Del Mar hesitated, and Marsden silently thanked him for keeping his head. While Murakame's strange vitals might be explained by a battle-induced injury, she had neglected to do anything in the background that would make it actually seem like they were being attacked. There were no bullets flying, no roar of explosions. They hadn't even powered up Dropship Alpha for flight yet, which would have been standard combat procedure under those circumstances.

Which was all pretty ironic. If Murakame had waited just a few minutes, Marsden and the remains of his group would have already provided them with exactly all that. Instead, now that del Mar's suspicion was up, it would hopefully stay up even in the ensuing chaos.

Assuming they all survived the initial distraction, that was. Marsden nodded at Axel. "Now."

The look on Axel's face was both priceless and disturbing. The term *kid in a candy store* was too tame for her expression, but there was no mistaking the sheer joy she felt at the prospect of the destruction she was about to cause. With a deep, appreciative sigh that was almost orgasmic, Axel mashed down on the detonator button.

For a few seconds nothing seemed to happen, and Marsden's hopes fell. Then there was a rumbling in the near distance and, despite warnings Axel had given them not to look at the ship, most of the team couldn't help but take a quick glance back before turning their heads and shielding their eyes.

The Sten-Plus vessel shook with several loud, high-pitched pops. There were several more seconds, then the front end of the ship erupted in a massive fireball. Like a wave, explosions moved backward over the ship. The spacecraft's hull rippled and tore as the explosion ripped through everything. Although there was some distance between them and the drop ships, Marsden could feel small, searing pieces of the ship flutter down around them.

The Thirty-Sevens ducked, completely caught off guard to suddenly be in exactly the situation they had just lied about to the *Dixon*. Perfect.

"Now!" Marsden yelled. "Take them out!" The remaining members of his team ran from their hiding spot with their weapons roaring. At this distance they weren't yet likely to get a direct hit on the Thirty-Sevens, but that wasn't exactly their goal just yet. All they really needed to do in this exact moment was cause damage. Many of the bullets hit the remaining blue stasis bubbles, and while many of them withstood the onslaught, several burst under the rain of ammunition and exposed the soft, fleshy parasites within. These suddenly became easy pickings as the Recon Marines moved closer.

Both Murakame and Singh ran inside the ship, although Marsden noticed that they did it in weird, backwards crab-walk. That made sense, Marsden realized. It didn't matter too much to the Thirty-Sevens if their host was damaged. There were other hosts out there, after all. But they couldn't risk any damage to the fleshy, tumor-like brains on their backs.

"Aim for the parasites themselves!" Marsden called. "That's their weak spots!" Nooner, instead of running for the safety of the ship, made a beeline for the weapons they had carelessly left sitting on the planet's surface.

"Marsden!" Essentia yelled.

"Not now, Essentia! We're a little busy!"

"No, listen! The signal on our PDMs is working again! We can contact the *Dixon*!"

Marsden ducked for the cover of a rock so he could check to see if what she said was true. Whatever it was that had been blocking their signal, whether it was something on the Sten-Plus ship or something the Thirty-Sevens had been doing themselves, now seemed to be gone. Marsden wasted no time broadcasting a signal to the *Franklin Dixon*.

"*Dixon*, this is Marsden! Do not, I repeat, do not listen to anything Murakame says. She, Nooner, and Singh are the ones that are currently infected by the parasites. You cannot let them board the *Franklin Dixon*! If you do—" His signal suddenly cut off again, and was then replaced by another image of Murakame.

"*Dixon*, they're trying to trick you! Marsden and those with him have been compromised! We are the only ones who haven't been infected. If Marsden makes any attempt to get back on the ship, you shoot him down!"

The *Franklin Dixon* didn't make any attempt to send back a message to either of them.

"Seems like the Dixon doesn't know which one of us to believe," Hemingford said. "Maybe we should—" His advice was cut off by a line of bullets punching him in the chest, going upward over his neck and turning his face into an unidentifiable ruin. The remaining marines doubled down their attempts on Nooner, who made the unfortunate move of turning just a little too much and exposing his parasite. Bayne got off several shots that shredded through the brain-like mass, and Nooner collapsed. Bayne made sure to keep firing into his body for several seconds just to make sure that the real Nooner wouldn't just lay there suffering.

In the midst of the firefight, the hatch on Dropship Alpha had begun to close. While there were still plenty of parasites sitting in their protective stasis bubbles on the ground, apparently Murakame had made the decision that the ones they had already taken aboard would be enough.

"Concentrate all fire on Dropship Alpha!" Marsden said. "Try to aim for the engines! We can't let them take off!"

Axel responded to this in the only way she knew how, by pulling out a grenade, ripping the pin out with her teeth, and then lobbing it with all her might in the direction of the dropship. Her aim was a little off and it missed the engine, but when the grenade went off it looked like some of the shrapnel got caught in the engine. The dropship began to hum, a clear sign that something had gone wrong in its engines, but it still managed to take off just as the hatch completely closed. It hovered in the air for a moment, rocking back and forth, and then slowly rose farther into the air.

As the ship rose out of their range of fire, Marsden, Axel, Bayne, and Essentia stopped shooting and looked balefully up at their escaping target.

"We failed," Essentia said. "They're getting away."

Marsden shook his head, then pointed at Dropship Beta, sitting forgotten off to the side. A couple of small, flaming pieces of the alien spacecraft had landed on it, but it looked to Marsden like it would still be able to fly.

"Not yet, they haven't."

August 2, 2147 (Earth Calendar)
2103 Greenwich Mean Time
Location: Interior of Dropship Beta, Bullfinch-2
Marine Heartbeats Detected on Planet: 4

Marsden entered Dropship Beta first and did a quick visual check to see if anything was outwardly wrong with it. The interior lights flickered, which could have been a result of damage from the falling debris, or it could have simply meant that some maintenance robot hadn't been quick enough to fix the fixtures before the ship had launched. Axel and Essentia were right behind him, with Bayne trailing far behind. Under other circumstances Marsden would have chided him for taking so long, but when Marsden looked back he saw that the big man had the bodies of Nooner and Hemingford draped over his shoulders. When possible, a Recon Marine tried not to leave the body of a comrade behind, and far too many marines today would not be headed back to Earth for a proper burial and funeral service. Given that Marsden couldn't have the ship take off until he did the most basic flight checks, he was more than willing to let Bayne take the extra time to do this the right way.

"How much time to we have to stop Alpha from reaching the *Dixon*?" Essentia asked.

"Average flight time of a dropship from takeoff to docking under non-emergency conditions is sixteen minutes, twenty-nine seconds, depending on weather," Axel said. "The current weather is fair, and Singh will be trying to push the ship to its limits, but we also need to factor in—"

"Axel, we don't have time for the full calculations," Marsden said as he ran to the pilot station and started flipping switches before he even sat down. "Just give us your best guess."

Axel sniffed, as though the entire concept of a "best guess" was offensive to her when she was on a roll, before she said, "Eighteen minutes, eleven seconds."

"That's just a guess?" Essentia asked incredulously.

"Yes."

As the engines whined to life, Bayne came through the open hatchway and deposited the two bodies as reverently as possible on the floor. He then frowned and went back further into the ship before coming back to them. "Hey guys? I think there's something you need to see."

"I'm kind of busy here at the moment," Marsden said. "Can't you just tell us whatever it is?"

"Sure. This ship is crawling with those brain parasite things."

"What?" Marsden risked wasting a small amount of time to rush back and see what Bayne was talking about. The way Bayne had said it, he'd expected the creatures to oozing around freely in the back of the troop hold just waiting for someone they could leap on and take over. Instead he found a small pile of the blue stasis bubbles. Apparently Murakame had managed to load a few into this ship as well before Marsden and the others had gotten out of the Sten-Plus ship. "Get them out of here," Marsden said. "Or at least as many any you can before takeoff. We don't want any live versions of these things on board the *Dixon*."

"Shouldn't we leave one or two to be studied by the Science Corps?" Essentia asked. "Anything they might be able to learn from them could be important to the survival of humanity if we ever encounter them again."

Marsden shook his head. "Think about it for a minute, Essentia. For one, we do in fact have a specimen for them to study. It's just not alive." Marsden indicated Nooner's bullet-ridden body and the mangled mass still attached to his back. "Second, while I certainly trust the Science Corps well enough, I don't trust the rest of humanity. If someone were to get their hands on just one of these things and try to use it as a weapon against some other human faction, imagine how quickly that could get out of hand. We still don't know how or how quickly these things reproduce. If the process is easy for them, humanity could still get wiped out purely by the Thirty-Sevens being used carelessly."

Essentia looked pained but nodded. While Essentia, Axel, and Bayne went about clearing the blue bubbles from the ship, Marsden went back to the pilot station and checked all the readouts. One of the wings had in fact been damaged by the explosion's debris, but the engines and fuel were in good order. This would not be a smooth ride at all, especially considering how far he needed to push the dropship beyond its suggested limits, but he thought he could do it. Successfully docking with the *Dixon* afterward could be a problem, but that assumed that they would even make it that far. Who knew? The *Franklin Dixon* might decide that Dropship Beta did in fact carry infected humans after all and just blow the dropship out of the sky. That was a fun thought, but not one he had time to worry about at the moment.

Once enough of the flight indicators were in the green, Marsden turned and called back to the others. "Is everything all set back there?" He couldn't immediately see them in the main troop hold, but there shouldn't have been any reason for them not to hear him. Despite this, they were silent.

No, strike that. Marsden did indeed hear something. It sounded like grunts.

It sounded like there was a struggle.

Marsden ran into the back as he pulled out a side arm with

one hand and a knife with the other. All but two of the blue spheres were gone, but those were forgotten for the moment. Essentia was face-down on the floor, struggling to get away as one of the parasites struggled directly over her. It was obvious to Marsden that the creature was trying to take its place on her back and begin the horrific bonding process, but both Axel and Bayne had their hands on the thing, trying to pull it back.

"Marsden, help!" Axel said. "Essentia somehow opened one of the bubbles while she was trying to roll it out the hatch."

"This sucker's stronger than it looks," Bayne grunted. The parasite had one of its tentacles suctioned on each side of Essentia, and it was trying to pull itself into position. Despite Bayne's enormous strength combined with Axel's health, the creature was gaining ground. From this angle, with the parasite not yet attached to Essentia's back, Marsden could see some kind of mouth-like structure on the underside. It was rimmed in sharp fangs to rip apart the flesh underneath, and a number of smaller tendrils lashed out from the opening. That would probably be what it used to get into the person's system once it had made a sizeable enough hole in the body.

Marsden swore and kneeled down next to them, deciding after a moment to set his side arm aside and just go with the knife. His pistol might be better at doing damage to the parasite, but there was too much risk of accidentally hurting one of the others in the process. And too many Recon Marines had already died today. He refused to let even one more go down under his watch.

"Please, you've got to swear," Essentia said in a soft, worried voice. "If it gets me, you have to kill me. Don't let me become like the others."

"You're not going to become like the others," Marsden said as he looked for the most likely place to stick his knife in the creature. The underside near the mouth looked the most vulnerable, although he didn't want any of the tendril to touch him.

The creature suddenly whipped a couple of its other small tentacles at all of them at once, causing Marsden to pull back. Both Bayne and Axel's grips slipped on the parasite's slimy skin, and the creature landed on Essentia's back.

"No!" Marsden yelled, immediately forgetting all thoughts of going after the creature with medical precision. Instead he repeatedly stabbed the creature, over and over.

Essentia screamed. It wasn't just the cry of someone who had been startled by something landing on her. It was the deep, true-pain scream of someone who could feel her back being ripped apart.

Bayne and Axel, no longer held back by trying to keep the parasite at bay, also pulled out their knives and hacked at the monstrosity. It was all over in a matter of seconds, but Marsden feared they were still too late. As Bayne and Marsden pulled the dead monster off Essentia, Axel took her PDM and checked Essentia's vital signs.

"Brainwave activity is still normal," Axel said. "It didn't get that far into her nervous system. Heart rate is elevated, but that's to be expected. She seems fine."

"Essentia, are you okay?" Marsden asked.

There was a long moment before Essentia replied. "I can't feel my legs."

Marsden hissed and took a closer look at the spot where the parasite had tried to invade Essentia's body. There was a ragged hole at the base of her spine that clearly showed cracked bone. Some kind of fluid was oozing out that Marsden was not familiar with. Axel identified it for them. "Spinal fluid. She needs a doctor immediately, or else she could risk permanent spinal damage."

"Axel, do your best to keep her from bleeding out for the moment and then strap her in. We're about to have a very bumpy ride, and I don't want it to do any further damage to her. Bayne, dump the last two spheres out the hatch. And hurry, both of you. Time's almost up."

Marsden couldn't afford to wait and make sure they'd done what he asked. He trusted them both to take care of their duties quickly and efficiently while he ran back to the pilot's chair, strapped himself in, did a final check on the dropship's status, and then lifted off from planet Bullfinch-2. He sincerely hoped he would never have to see this useless ball of rock ever again.

"Everyone brace yourselves," Marsden called back to the others. "I'm about to do some really stupid things."

He pushed forward on one control stick and pulled back on the other fast enough that, if he'd still been with his old instructor back in training, the instructor would have berated him for putting everyone in danger and then stuck him with a full month's worth of cleaning duties. Marsden didn't have the luxury of being safe and by the book, though. He did some quick mental calculations. Axel had given the first dropship about eighteen minutes to reach the *Dixon* in its current condition. They'd just had to use about eight or nine minutes prepping the ship, clearing it out, and saving Essentia.

He had less than ten minutes to reach Alpha before it docked at the *Dixon*. That seemed impossible, but he was the master of winning the impossible bet. He had to do some things to put the odds back in his favor.

"Axel!" he called back. "Get on the ship's comm system and try to contact the *Dixon*. Do everything you can to convince them that we're the ones who are uninfected."

"On it!"

"Bayne, get your ass up here and get into the co-pilot's seat."

"Uh, I can't walk in this ship when you're flying like that. And I don't know how to co-pilot."

"Quit being such a baby. And I don't want you to co-pilot, I want you to take control of the weapons systems on this thing. I can't try to shoot at the other ship and put it through idiotic maneuvers at the same time!"

Bayne grunted. "Fine." The ship's erratic movements caused him to bounce around against the walls before he finally made it to the co-pilot's seat. He didn't perk up until he sat down in his chair and saw what he had to work with. "Oooh. I didn't know these things were equipped with a Winchester '43 Gatling System. I've always wanted to play with one of these."

"Then now's your chance, big guy," Marsden said. "Although I would strap in first. Everyone else in this ship is going to do a whole lot of cursing at me before I'm through with this."

He could hear Axel trying to hail the *Dixon* from behind them, and urging the *Dixon* crew to make Murakame show them her back before they would let her dock. Judging from the pause after this, Marsden guessed that she followed this up by pointing the camera at her own back. Very clever, but given the way she had to repeat the message over and over, Marsden wasn't sure if she was getting through to the troop transport, and he didn't have a spare moment to check, either. Several of the gauges in front of him went from green to yellow as they told him that he was pushing the ship to a speed that it had never been built to handle. Things were made all the more complicated by the damaged wing, which caused the entire dropship to shimmy worryingly the more he pushed it to its limits.

As the purple sky of the planet's atmosphere gave way to the darker blue and then black of space, Marsden saw the other dropship appear on his instruments. A quick scan told him that the ship was moving even slower than they had guessed. Either the damage had been more extensive than it looked, or the parasite infecting Singh still hadn't pulled all the information needed from the marine's brain to fly the ship properly. Either way, it meant that Marsden's odds were getting better here.

A message came over the ship's system. "Dropships Alpha and Beta, this is del Mar on the *Franklin Dixon*. You are both ordered to cease your approach of the *Dixon* and hold your current orbit until we can properly assess the current threat level. Do you read?"

Marsden grimaced. He was sure that the *Dixon* would turn its weapons on them if they didn't comply, but he wasn't sure that he was comfortable following the order while Alpha still made its approach. "Axel, tell the *Dixon* that as Dropship Alpha is the closer of the two of us, we will only comply if we see that Alpha is complying first." He waited to hear what Alpha might say in response, but there was nothing from the other dropship. Instead, Marsden's instruments told him that Alpha sped up.

"They know the game is up," Marsden said. "They're probably going to try some desperate move like crashing through the *Dixon*'s airlock to get the parasites inside. Bayne, I hope you're ready with those weapons."

"Hell yeah, I'm ready!"

Marsden pushed the controls harder. The ship shuddered and made several very worrying noises from the direction of the engines. Multiple gauges in front of Marsden went from yellow to red, flashing a bright "Warning!" light that several of the ship's systems were now in dangerous territory. But the distance between them and Dropship Alpha continued to shorten, and

Marsden could now see the other dropship for ahead of them against the backdrop of space.

He could also see a speck that he identified as the *Franklin Dixon*. And if the two ships could see each other, that meant that they were now in range of the *Dixon*'s weapons.

"Bayne, can you get a lock on Alpha yet?" Marsden asked.

"Still too far away. You have to get us closer."

"Seriously? What do think I've already been trying to do here, bake snickerdoodles?"

"Aw, you had to go and mention snickerdoodles. Now I'm hungry."

"Focus, Bayne!"

The dark sky lit up as the *Franklin Dixon* started firing on Dropship Alpha. Alpha juked from side to side, dodging the majority of the fire, although it looked like some of the ammo might have clipped it. Dropship Alpha got noticeably wobbly. Marsden took advantage of that as he continued to push Beta beyond its limits.

"Marsden, something's smoking back here!" Axel called. "I think you might have blown the auxiliary synergy link!"

"See if there's anything you can do to stabilize it," Marsden replied. "I can't pull back now!"

"Alpha will be in range in twenty seconds," Bayne said. Ahead of them, Dropship Alpha's movements became more erratic as it did its desperate best to get through the Dixon's volley. According to Marsden's instruments, at this rate Dropship Alpha would be able to make it to the *Dixon* and punch through into the ship bay in roughly fifteen seconds.

Marsden pushed the ship harder, trying to make up the deficit. Something small sounded like it exploded in the rightmost engine. Immediately two of the gauges went from red to complete black to indicate that their systems had gone into shutdown. It was only one engine though. He still had three more, although every one of them looked like they were going to join the first engine in any second.

"Range is dropping," Bayne said. "Alpha will be in our range in only three, two..."

Bayne never waited for one. He immediately let loose with the weapons systems, focusing all of the dropship's fire onto Alpha.

Their shots hit something vital in Dropship Alpha's rear. It wobbled erratically for a moment, then exploded.

Marsden's first impulse was to celebrate, but as Beta crashed through Alpha's debris field, he realized they and the *Dixon* were still in danger. Dropship Beta was now headed directly for the *Dixon* at a ludicrous speed. Marsden pulled up, but the previous damage to the wing and the additional damage they had received flying through the remains of the Alpha affected his ability to change course.

"The *Dixon* is re-aiming to target us," Bayne said.

"*Dixon*, this is Dropship Beta. Do not fire!" Axel yelled into the comm system. "I repeat, do not fire! We are not infected!"

Marsden grimaced at the force with which he had to yank back on the controls. The *Dixon* began firing, but they were too close and going too fast for the troop transport to hit them. Marsden watched the screen as the Dixon got closer and closer, yet also lower with each passing second. If he could only... just... keep... holding back... on the controls...

There was a slight screech as the bottom of Dropship Beta barely scraped against the top of the *Dixon*, and then they were over and past it. Several more of the red gauges went dark in front of him, but more of them dropped from red to yellow, then yellow to green, as Marsden finally let the ship slow down and come to a halt.

"Dropship Beta, this is del Mar on the *Franklin Dixon*," del Mar said over their communications channel. "Our instruments are telling us that there are four people onboard, and that none show the vital signs that were supposedly evident for this parasitic infection. Can you confirm this?"

Marsden finally addressed del Mar himself using his PDM. "*Dixon*, we can confirm this. Essentia is badly wounded, though, and needs immediate medical attention."

"Affirmative, Marsden. We will allow Dropship Beta to board once we have done a thorough scan and sweep of your ship to insure that everything is as you say it is. Given the circumstances, I'm sure you can appreciate our caution."

Marsden let out a long sigh, all the tension that had been building up in his body finally leaving. "Roger that, *Dixon*." He paused, then added, "And holy crap, do we ever have some stories to tell you."

August 3, 2147 (Earth Calendar)
0106 Greenwich Mean Time
Location: Troop Transport Franklin Dixon, near Bullfinch-2
Marine Heartbeats Detected on Ship: 11

Their debriefing took longer than the time they had actually been on the planet.

Essentia, as she had to immediately be carted off to the med bay in the hopes of saving what remained of her spine, was the only one who didn't have to go through the grueling process. First Marsden, Bayne, and Axel had been forced to go over everything as a group, repeating it all to one of the commanding marines who had been lucky enough to stay on board the ship. Then each one of them had needed to go over their stories individually. After that, there had been the tech report where they'd had to go over the data they'd gathered and saved into their PDMs. Then they all had to go over the story *again*, this time with their interviewer asking pointed questions on everything from their decisions on which bodies to leave behind to exactly how bad Hairy had smelled. All the while they'd been continually poked and prodded by a doctor, who checked for everything from alien viruses to whether their heartbeats and reflexes were responding normally. Finally, only after it was all done, were they allowed to go into the mess hall to eat.

As Marsden sat down at his table with a tray of synthetic chicken and rice, he couldn't help but feel like the room was eerily quiet. Those marines who had stayed on the ship had eaten much earlier, and most of them were sleeping in normal bunks waiting to be woken up just so they could be put into dilation-sleep. That meant that there were only three occupants in the entire mess hall. The last time Marsden had been in here, it had been full of his comrades.

Comrades who were gone. Comrades who, with the exception of Hemingford and Nooner, would not be receiving anything resembling a proper burial. Even Nooner might not get such a thing, given that the monstrosity latched to his back made him a scientific curiosity that the Science Corps would not easily give up.

Marsden hadn't been close to most of them. It was a survival habit that had been drilled into him through years of service in the Recon Marines. The job of a marine was tough, tougher than any civilian could possibly comprehend, and it meant that there were always a few on most missions that didn't come home.

But this. This was beyond anything he had ever seen. It didn't matter that he hadn't exactly considered any of the missing marines his friends. They had still been his brothers and sisters. And so many of them were now gone without a trace.

Axel set her tray down next to him. Shortly afterward, Bayne did the same. For a long time all three of them ate their tasteless food in peace. Marsden finally broke the silence by saying, "Do either of you know anything about Essentia's condition?"

"They still don't know whether she'll ever be able to walk again," Axel said with uncharacteristic solemnness. "There might be some treatments that will help her, but the Thirty-Seven completely ravaged the base of her spinal column. It's going to take more than just run-of-the-mill stem cell therapy."

"I'm going to love it when I can finally go to sleep," Bayne said. "Who knew that talking to a bunch of pencil-necks for hours could be so draining?"

"And we're going to have to do more of it when we get

back," Marsden said. "Hell, they might even make us have a personal meeting with Mister himself. The knowledge we have now is valuable."

"I don't know," Bayne said. "Maybe not. Maybe the Sten-Plus aren't really a threat. Maybe this whole mess is just going to be a one-off incident."

Marsden glared at him. "Really? You want to bet?"

"No," both Axel and Bayne said at the same time.

They all looked at each other and laughed. They had to, because the only other option would have been to cry. And they couldn't allow themselves to do that. They were Recon Marines.

End

CHECK OUT OTHER GREAT SCIENCE FICTION BOOKS

DERELICT: MARINES
by **Paul E. Cooley**

Fifty years ago, Mira, humanity's last hope to find new resources, exited the solar system bound for Proxima Centauri b. Seven years into her mission, all transmissions ceased without warning. Mira and her crew were presumed lost. Humanity, unified during her construction, splintered into insurgency and rebellion.

Now, an outpost orbiting Pluto has detected a distress call from an unpowered object entering Sol space: Mira has returned. When all attempts at communications fail, S&R Black, a Sol Federation Marine Corps search and rescue vessel, is dispatched from Trident Station to intercept, investigate, and tow the beleaguered Mira to Neptune.

As the marines prepare for the journey, uncertainty and conspiracy fomented by Trident Station's governing AIs, begin to take their toll. Upon reaching Mira, they discover they've been sent on a mission that will almost certainly end in catastrophe.

ALLIANCE MARINES
by **John Mierau**

One by one, all of Earth's colonies have gone dark and silent. Reach, the last colony, teeters on the verge of civil war against its Earth-loyal overlords...and Reach-born rebel Lee Zhang has sworn to push the planet over the edge.

As the colony descends into total war, a convoy from Earth races across the galaxy, carrying news of a threat unlike anything mankind has faced before. The colonies have all been destroyed by a vast alien horde, and now Earth has fallen, too. Time is running out for sworn enemies to learn to trust and unite, or the human race is extinct. The Takers are coming to destroy mankind. If we don't do the job for them first.

CHECK OUT OTHER GREAT SCIENCE FICTION BOOKS

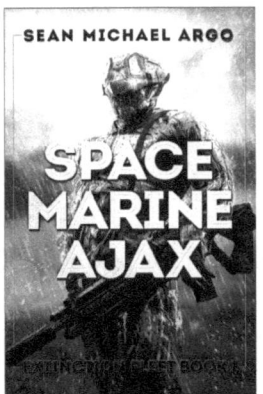

CHECK OUT OTHER GREAT
SCIENCE FICTION BOOKS

ROAK
by Jake Bible

There are thousands of bounty hunters across the galaxy. Solid professionals that take jobs based on the credits the bounties afford. They follow the letter of the law so they can maximize those credits.

Licensed, bonded, legal.

Then there's Roak.

Deadly, unstoppable, invisible.

SIEGE
by Gustavo Bondoni

This is humanity's last stand. Threatened on all sides by enemies they can't fight and often can't even comprehend, the human race has taken refuge in an inhospitable corner of the galaxy. A tiny pocket of habitable space concealed by black holes and dust clouds, hiding a cluster of colonies where the last humans in the galaxy reside, preparing themselves for a war of annihilation against all comers. Crystallia is a hidden military base that guards the access route to the colonies. The main mission of the soldiers there is to remain undetected for as long as possible, to spot any incursions from the outside and to hit them with everything in humanity's arsenal. No one is quite convinced that this strategy will be enough to save the colonies or even to create enough of a delay for some of the colonists to escape. The best bet for the human race is to remain concealed. Unfortunately, something has found them.

www.ingramcontent.com/pod-product-compliance
Lightning Source LLC
Chambersburg PA
CBHW051959170626
46808CB00007B/2687